Precious Little Life

Charlie Bowles

This is a work of fiction. Names, characters, places, and incidents either are the product of the author's imagination or are used fictitiously. Any resemblance to actual persons, living or dead, events, or locales is entirely coincidental.

Copyright © 2020 by Charlie Bowles

All rights reserved. No part of this book may be reproduced in any form on by an electronic or mechanical means, including information storage and retrieval systems, without permission in writing from the publisher, except by a reviewer who may quote brief passages in a review.

First paperback edition December 2020

Book cover design by Charlie Bowles

ISBN 979-8-5822-8664-6

Published independently by Charlie Bowles
www.charliebowlesnovelist.co.uk

To my family, friends and partner for your love, support and encouragement.

CHAPTER 1
Silent Night

This was the first time that Kaira Johnstone had been separated from her mother and had not felt the need to cry.

Winter had arrived, fashioned in Christmas décor and starlit by the bountiful use of fairy lights. Festivities beckoned people across the world to the captivating streets of Scotland's capital: Edinburgh.

Neon colours danced along the outline of the Ferris wheel, casting its rainbow silhouette on the Walter Scott Monument; the jagged Gothic spire that pierced the sky. The public indulged in all the joy to be had; from ice skating and scenic mazes to dizzying themselves on the merry-go-round; after a few too many cups of mulled wine.

Paramount to all these festivities was the most anticipated yearly attraction: the Christmas Market.

This is where four and a half-year-old Kaira Johnstone had found herself lost.

While she was very much aware of where she was, she was even more aware that she was there alone and had no clue how to return home. Yet, despite not knowing where her mother, her father, or her two older brothers were, she wasn't frightened or sad. The calmness she felt came from a senseless certainty that nothing and no-one could hurt her.

She couldn't feel anything anymore. The cold had ceased to pinch her cheeks long ago and her billowy cream coat had lost its cosy touch moments after. Scents of the simmering delicacies had now evaporated. The excited chatter of the crowd had been reduced to a faint humming. The lights that twinkled brightly, on every tree and every stall, had blurred into luminous baubles that floated between faceless figures, shining over them like halos.

Among the murmuring white noise, Kaira's little ears caught hold of a tune. To her muffled hearing, the words were incomprehensible but the melody of Silent Night was unmistakable. Somewhere, not too far from her, a choir was singing. A memory returned to her vague and fragmented; that choir had been singing cheerier Christmas songs earlier. Silent Night was hardly her favourite song; the bittersweet sound always had a wistful effect on her, but hearing it at that moment made her happy. It was familiar.

As the music continued to soothe her, one thing broke through the blurry barrier in perfect clarity. At the opposite end of the makeshift street of stalls, there stood a man. Layers of knitwear were bunched under his grey coat, which looked as though it had scarcely survived the last winter, and his chin rested on a thick tattered scarf. His ragged appearance reminded her of her teddy bear, despite his sallow face and tired eyes.

While the faceless figures around them paid no attention to her, his direct stare made her feel as though the entire world were her audience, waiting for her to say or do something. She had a sense that this man was stranger than any stranger she had come across, but he didn't scare her. She felt comfortable in his spotlight; his presence made her happy. He felt familiar.

Kaira approached the strange man without her usual shyness or reluctance. Excitement urged her to greet him; as if he were a beloved relative visiting for the holidays. As she drew nearer, the stranger kneeled down to her height. Through strands of ashen hair, a kindness emitted from his eyes.

'Did you enjoy it here?' he asked softly.

'Yeah, lots!' Kaira said in delight. She could not feel the movement of her lips as she spoke; the words seemed to spill straight out of her mind.

The man took her hands delicately; as though she was made of snow and would crumble at the touch of his fingertips.

A sympathetic tone came with his second question, 'You know you have another home, right?'

She nodded. Despite never being told this piece of knowledge, the feeling of certainty was so strong that there was no trace of doubt. What he said was true.

'Would you like to go back to your other home?'

She paused, just for a moment, sparing a thought for all those she would leave behind. They would catch up to her, one day, when it was time. For now, she wanted to go to a place where everything was clear and familiar; a place she would no longer be lost, the place she knew he wanted to take her.

'Yes please.' She smiled at him.

It was the same happy and beloved smile that had been captured in the many photos that decorated her family's house. Photos that hung on the walls; of her being kissed on either cheek by her brothers; of her dressed as a fairy with chocolate smudged across her mouth; of her wedged between the affection of her grandparents. Photos that sat on side tables; of her and her mother paddling in a pool; of her forcing her father to join her toys in a tea party; of her clinging to her teddy bear. The background on her father's phone; of her with her family at the Christmas Market, just a few days ago.
In that same moment, photos just like those were scattered across the carpet of her parent's bedroom. The one currently clutched in her mother's hands; she was not smiling, she had not learned how to yet. In the picture, she was only hours old and in the arms of her

mother, who beamed brightly through tears and exhaustion. A baby, unaware of all the joy life would bring to her, and all the joy she had brought to the world from the second she was born.

The man invited her into his arms and Kaira Johnstone threw herself into them gladly. A bright light pushed out from within her, wiping away the outline of her existence and enveloping everything that surrounded her. Warmth radiated through him, and in one moment he experienced four and a half years' worth of blissful happiness. Though he couldn't witness her memories, he could feel each one relive itself within him.

Regardless of how short it was, Kaira Johnstone had a wonderful life.

The light shrunk back into itself, fading in an instant. She was gone. As the man stood up, his complexion had paled even further, his smile had faded and all kindness had vanished from his eyes. He pulled down the sleeve of his coat to reveal a list written from his wrist downwards; Neil MacGowan, Shona Gibson, Nadia Roshan, Gary Hughes, Kaira Johnstone. The first four had a score through each of them. With one nail, he scratched out the last. A dim silver light outlined the ink of each letter of each name before the list melted into his skin.

The faceless figures perceived by the little girl began to take notice of the strange man's presence among them. His perfect vision could see their faces clearly and every little detail of disgust they expressed. Although they were not consciously aware of it, their basic instincts could feel who he was; and what he did.

While Kaira experienced a calm familiarity, their flesh-bound existence saw horror and felt dread. Suspicious glances judged him as dangerous. Their ignorance was incurable; if he could speak the truth they wouldn't believe it.

He briskly left the charming market, that was quickly losing its charm, and hurried up steps that would lead him away from the crowds and up The Mound. Dodging heavy glares and hostile stares from passersby, he scurried across the street. He returned the hostility with his fiercest scowl before diving into a dimly lit walkway. This job was making him bitter.

More steps led him to a quiet courtyard. Residential buildings loomed over, sheltering him from the city that currently despised him. Their worn and darkened bricks told tales of centuries past, with paned windows that stared vacantly upon him. A singular street lamp, that had seen at least a century itself, stood tall in the centre, emanating a soft silver light that made the walls appear frostier than they actually were.

Wise words from historic writers were engraved across slabs, ready to be walked over by people too busy to heed them, but not at that moment. They knew not to come now. They would stare into the darkness and sense the shadows staring back, threatening them to stay away.

Waiting patiently under the light, there was a figure. It hovered over the ground, appearing as a shadow, shrouded in frayed frostbitten fabric. Its only solid attribute was its fleshless, spindly hands.

The strange man greeted Death with an arched brow and a deep resentful sigh, 'We've got to find a better way of communicating. I can't have you making me reek of death every time you need me. I wouldn't be surprised if I got lynched next time.'

Death presented one skeletal hand then the other, gesturing that their options were limited.

'These mobile things are pretty handy, think it's time you learned to text.'

Death moved its hand through the lamp post, the form of its bony fingers rippled like water.

'Yeah, it's no that I forgot. Just thought you might have learned an alternative method, some point in the last... how many centuries?'

The figure was still. Its hooded shadow glaring more unnervingly than eyes were capable of doing.

Defeated, he turned away, 'So how many names this time?'
Death raised one osseous finger. The sight of it hooked the man's peripheral vision, slowly reeling his head back around to face the spectre again. He was struck with the same feeling he had given to those he had passed by: dread.

His balance abandoned him; he was forced to lean against the nearest wall while preparing himself for the one name. As moments past with his eyes fixated on Death's finger, he became increasingly aware of the fear that grew inside him. He wasn't ready.

Nevertheless, he composed himself and stepped forward dutifully. Death began to move again, caressing the air in front of it, casting sparks in the air as if its finger was a lit match. Silver flames blossomed in front of the man's eyes, burning letters of the same colour into the air.

A sudden wave of relief crashed upon him, washing away every last speck of distress; it was not the name he had feared. He struggled to make out the letters, but there were far too many to be the name he had assumed it to be.

The flames gradually relented, declaring the name in visible steel letters:

"Haidee McLean."

CHAPTER 2
Ding Dong Merrily On High

The smoke tried to slither out from her throat, searing her tonsils and tongue. A second breath invited a soothing breeze that banished the smoke deep down into the depths of her lungs. Heat danced inside her chest as she tried to hold it captive for as long as possible; with her mouth closed, the hot mist escaped from her nostrils, shivering out of existence as it plunged into the November air. Any stress, anger or upset she had felt that day was now drifting away from her, replaced by surreal bliss. It was a herbal remedy, a massage for the mind: marijuana.

'Oi, Dee, geis a puff?' Leah waved over, with a polystyrene chippy box in one hand and a drunk bloke steadying himself in the other.

'Enjoy.' Haidee held out the joint as her friend came clunking towards her in fashionable stilts.

Leah took a quick breath of it, choked immediately, then in a nursing manner, brought the burning stick to her new found pet's lips. He inhaled the smoke and exhaled it slowly. Although his eyes were only visible through slits, he appeared to be content.

'Whaddya think ay him?' Leah grinned boastfully.

Having had just the one drink, Haidee felt sober enough to be a fair judge of this man as her friend's new love interest. Despite his shirt sampling some curry sauce, he seemed well dressed and his face had a somewhat boyish charm, in that obliviously drunk sort of way. He spat out an unintelligible string of words, that possibly translated into a sentence about Leah being sexy, and then started rambling on about how curly Haidee's hair was.

'Well, he's conscious.' She smiled, unsure of what else to say.

Leah scooped her intoxicated companion into her bosom and winked cheekily at Haidee, 'That's aw he needs t'be!'

The match made in margaritas headed toward the endless queue for taxis that were coming and going like bees busy in a hive. Incidentally, The Hive was the name of the club of which they had been to. Haidee couldn't call the club her scene, but the drinks were cheap, and beggars can't be choosers.

Having had enough bartending experience to deal with the drunks that plagued the early hours of Saturday mornings and enough gumption to bring a pair of pumps to change into, she began to walk home.

The frost lay down a glittering silver carpet for her to walk across. Each breath in felt like ice sliding down into every branch of her lungs, freezing and restricting the movement of her chest. Each breath out warmed her mouth, tasting of weed and clouding her vision with the fog that tumbled out from her lips.

She shivered as she passed all the rides and stalls on Princes Street; closed up, turned off and abandoned for the night. She tiptoed around a small shrine of condolences mounted up against the iron fence. The frost had eaten away at most of the flowers and the afternoon rain had soaked every candle, soft toy and sympathy card. Words of grief had transformed into ink stains. The cards said nothing but showed overwhelming amounts of love just by being there. It was an eerie and hopeless sight, one she rushed by.

The streetlamps and the window displays of Princes Street's stores were the only sources of light revealing her surroundings. Each frame had a peek into the winter season of fashion, decorated with giant sparkling gift boxes, snowflakes, candy canes and any other Christmas prop they could throw in there.

A shimmer in the corner of her eye drew her gaze to the Debenhams store window. Amidst a jungle of oddly shaped baubles, there posed a mannequin dressed in a top that had Haidee's name all over it.

As she moved towards it, her reflection began to materialise; a ghostly apparition of her likeness painted itself over the mannequin. She watched her mirror image as the fraying six-year-old blouse she wore vanished into the deep blue sequins, which caught the light and shone in every direction. A smile grew on her face as the blue glow lit up her face. It was a glimpse into the life she could have one day, a possible version of herself who went to lavish cocktail bars after securing another client at her website design business. That top was for someone who didn't have to pick the cheapest drink off the menu and could enjoy a night out without instantly regretting the money spent. That top was for someone who could satisfy their desires within an instant, and not be kept wanting and wishing and waiting until "someday". Someday, when she had a career. Someday, when she could feel in control. Someday, when she could be beautiful. Someday, when she could afford more than a can of soup for dinner.

She took a few steps back and her reflection faded away. There was no point imaging herself into a Scottish Cinderella when Fairy Godmothers did not exist. She would have to try harder, and be much more frugal to finally reach that *someday*.

The drink that had cost her three whole pounds- which looked like nail polish remover, tasted like nail polish remover and probably was nail polish remover- was a regretful purchase weighing on her mind. With those three pounds, she could have had bolognese sauce and pasta. It wouldn't last long but at least it would have been filling.

The hazy calm of the spliff was obviously wearing off, letting the stresses of reality back through, but she had just the single joint as a present from her very generous friend, Matthew.

All she could do was wait until the end of next week, when her bank account would have a whole ten pounds sitting in it and her overdraft will have been defeated- at least for a few days. Her new job of handing out leaflets in the cold was far from ideal, but it would eventually pay for a soup-free living.
Amidst her anguish, a sudden sensation, a pang of panic, pierced through her thoughts. She whipped her head around, looking over her shoulder. Her eyes scanned over every shadow, every shape, every little detail of her surroundings.

There was nobody there.

But every nerve in her body told her otherwise.

She could feel it in the centre of her gut, somebody was standing in the exact spot to which her eyes were now fixed. Right in front of her. A conflict started between her senses; her heart told her that her eyes were lying, her eyes told her that her heart was mistaken and her brain reminded her that she was still stoned. Regardless of what the truth was, she sped up her pace.

Focusing her eyes on the distant church that marked the end of Princes Street, she was entirely hell-bent on running away from the nagging feeling in the back of her mind- so much so, that she hadn't noticed her feet beginning to slide over black ice. She had ignored the red man's light cautioning her as she stepped out onto the road, thinking it unnecessary at this time, when there were very few vehicles around.

Then- her right foot began to slip away from its original step. Her left foot pushed too hard on the ground, dragging her leg forward as it began to skate ahead. She threw her torso onwards- in pursuit of creating a steady balance- but both feet gave way, forcing her to fall face first.

Ice-glazed tar stung at her palms, cheeks and knees, pressing a groan out from her chest. All warmth from her body was being drained from the ice, and the pain kept her pinned to it. She attempted to push herself up with all her strength, but her muscles refused to move. They were still adjusting to their new damage, registering aches that would map out future bruises. She nestled into the frost, weeping tears of self-pity as she decided to rest in the middle of the road. Just for a few moments. Just until she could recover some strength.

There was no time.

A noise, a humming then a growling, pricked her ears up. Panicked, she spun her head around to see exactly what she feared it would be: a car, heading her way.
It came down The Mound, round the bend, too fast for her to listen to every fibre of her being screaming at her to move. The headlights blinded, not only her eyes but her thoughts, freezing at this one last message to herself: *I'm a fucking idiot.*

A screech shredded through the quiet night like a banshee. Haidee held her breath, trembling and waiting for the feeling of immense pain to hit her.

It did not.

It took a few moments for her to register the two bulky shadows breaking the car's glaring light. It was a pair of legs. Not just any legs. She recognised these legs, and as she scanned upwards, she recognised the person that they were attached to.

Her friend, Matthew, had stepped in front of the car. His hands were stretched out in a command for the vehicle to stop.

The driver opened the car door with a mobile at his ready, 'That girl awright?'

'I dunno. She slipped on the ice.' Matthew crouched down beside her and started to pull her up, 'You okay, Haidee?'

She winced, steadying her feet on the ground and putting all her weight onto him, 'Yeah, yeah, a bit sore but...'

'Want me to call an ambulance?' asked the driver, waving the mobile in his hand.

'Nah, I'm good.' Her groan was less than convincing, 'Just a few scrapes.' She hobbled to the pavement with Matthew's assistance.

The driver waved them over, 'Right, get in, I'll drive yous home.'

Matthew started to thank him and moved Haidee towards the car, she dug her heels in.

'I'm literally five minutes from my flat.'she protested.

Matthew cringed, 'Are you actual insane? You're injured!'

'I'm planning on gettin' sleep tonight,' the driver urged them over again, 'I cannae do that if I'm worrying about you.'

Matthew stared Haidee down with a concerned look, guilting her into overcoming her pride. She agreed, reluctantly.

After a one-minute drive, filled with awkward chit-chat, the driver dropped them both outside Haidee's flat. Despite Haidee insisting she was fine, Matthew was determined to see her to her door, right on the top floor of a four-storey building.

'I'm desperate for the loo.' he proclaimed halfway up the stairs, 'Mind if I come in for a minute?'

A pang of dread.
'Uh... My place is a bit of a tip at the moment.'

He raised one brow, 'Uh-huh, what's new?'

They shared a laugh, but Haidee's was clearly forced.

'You hiding a dead body?'

'Yeah.' She tried to joke, 'Finally rid us of that bagpiper, but they spawned a new one.'

'Damn.'

'I know.'

Upon reaching the door, her movements became stiff. She turned and hugged Matthew, 'Thank you for coming to my rescue.'
'No bother. Lemme use the loo and we're even.'

As she pulled back, he could read the anxiety on her face. She hesitantly unlocked the door, 'Like I said, it's a tip. Don't judge...'

The door dragged along the carpet, as reluctant to open as Haidee was to open it. Matthew didn't understand at first, with a flick of the light switch he could see into the hall and living room; neat, clean, exceptionally tidy- especially for Haidee. Then, he stepped in.
He could see each breath leave his and Haidee's mouths. Moistness clung to the wallpaper, curling it in the corners. Spots of mould dotted the carpet and wooden bookcase. The air was as damp and musty as the Edinburgh Dungeons.

The horror in his eyes filled her with shame, no concern for her own wellbeing, just wallowing in her utter failure to look after herself.

'When was the last time you had the heating on?' he asked.

The last time she had it on was the last time she could afford it, well over a month ago, but she would not say that. Instead she just shrugged.

'I need to...' He pointed, walking past her to the bathroom and slammed the door.

It was a struggle preparing herself for the confrontation she knew was imminent. Both the cold and anxiety had her hands shaking. She had managed to keep the poor condition of her living state a secret until now, knowing that if anyone was to find out they would challenge her capability to live on her own.

The toilet flushed loudly, interrupting Haidee's whirling thought and Matthew came out soon after, scratching his temple and cautiously treading towards Haidee.
After a long moment of silence, and a deep breath in, he said, 'Pack your stuff. You're coming to mine.'

She shook her head, 'I'm fine here-'

'Dee, it's an igloo in here. You're gonna catch pneumonia.'

'I won't. I don't mind the cold, and it'll only be like this until payday.'

Twitches of frustration pulled at his brows and lips. He placed a hold on her shoulders, as if to pull her back down to earth, 'Please, just come to mine. You can have my bed, I'll take the couch.'

'I can look after myself,' she refused to be a burden, 'I just had a wee dip. I've had to pay the rent myself since I split up with Ben. But I've got this new job, it pays ten pound an hour, I'll be fine in no time.'

'But right now, you're not! For all the times you helped me, please just let me help you, at least this once.'

He pleaded with his eyes, forcing her to break eye contact with him. She loved her flat, her own space, having control of her own life. It was something she had worked tirelessly for, the ability to rely on herself. To give that up, even for a night, she would feel like a failure.

'If I feel like I'm struggling, I'll tell you.' she lied.

He rolled his eyes, 'I love you, Dee, but that bloody... Pride of yours! Please, just come to mine!'

'You practically live in Musselburgh! And I have to get up for work early tomorrow.' Another lie, her next shift wasn't until the day after, 'I'm okay, I swear.'

He shook his head, 'Please just... Ask for help when you need it, okay?'

She smiled and nodded, before seeing him to the door. In one last attempt to make her see sense, he pleaded again, before realising that she was already resolved to stay.

Even after Matthew had left, the anxiety lingered. Even when she was nestled under her five duvets, the cold clung to her. Silence spoke to her in little unnerving paranoid thoughts. The darkness twisted the silhouettes of her furniture into shapes and outlines of what appeared to be a person.

She still couldn't shake the feeling; someone was watching her.

CHAPTER 3
In the Bleak Midwinter

Be approachable. Be confident. Be enthusiastic.

These things would be easier to *be* if it wasn't for the high-level gale, pushing sleet down Haidee's less-than-effective waterproof jacket. The force of the wind kept bending her arm back, as she reached out to the crowd of Princes Street, pleading for them to take her leaflets before the frosted raindrops gnawed through the paper.

Her desperate gaze darted from person to person as they hurried passed her with their eyes shut tight. She tried to tell herself this was to prevent the horrid predicament of sleet in their eyes but, she knew all too well, it was to prevent the horrid predicament of being stopped by her. Each rejection chipped away at her morale.

Standing her ground firmly against the Narnian gust, gripping her drenched leaflets, her smile froze into a chattering toothy cringe while she attempted to gesture to a man ducking under his umbrella.

His attention had been captured, much to her misfortune, as his drookit face flared in rage, 'Naeb'dy wants yer bloody soggy shite!'

There was a part of her that wanted to shout back. Scream back. Shove her soggy leaflets down his throat- but that wasn't Haidee. She was patient and polite, hard working and diligent. Unfortunately, this new job was less about hard work and more about endurance, and as the tears on her cheeks indicated, she was struggling to endure.

The wind and rain joined forces to defeat the already weakened durability of the leaflets, tearing them and the last of her morale apart. She scraped up the mush of word art and stock images off the pavement and proceeded to shuffle her feet towards the nearest bin, where she threw away the last piece of tolerance she had for the day and allowed herself an unauthorised break.

Sitting in a state of surrealism, warmth gradually returned to her fingers through the mug of freshly brewed hot chocolate. The cafe did well as a shelter from the bleak weather. People around her chatted away, reading their newspapers and typing on their laptops, while she simply gazed out the window, enjoying the view of Edinburgh Castle.

The clouds had descended into a mist, draining the life and colour from the city. It was as if she was staring at a century-old photo, black and white, hazed and grainy, and hauntingly beautiful. Then, her own haunting continued.

There were a pair of eyes on her, she was as certain of that feeling as she was of the warmth from her mug. Nervously, she took a quick glance around. Most people had their eyes fixed to a screen, or on their companion as they sipped and slurped their hot beverages. Then she spotted an older woman, sitting only a table over, fiddling with a small silver crucifix that hung around her neck, flicking flashes of light in her direction. As Haidee made eye contact, a large grin spread across the woman's face with the friendliest of intentions but the creepiest of impressions. Haidee twitched a smile back, trying to mask her discomfort. It was an odd thing she had noticed throughout her life: that religious folk, of any faith, always took an interest in her. Perhaps they could sense how pitiful her life was and their small piece of kindness was a good deed for the day.

The awkward eye contact was mercifully broken when a man took the seat opposite her. He casually put down his coffee, crossed his legs and started reading a newspaper. He looked worse than she did. His mesh of black hair was sodden wet and the cold had chapped his lips and pinkened his skin. She didn't mean to stare and wasn't completely aware that she was until he caught her in the act.

'Sorry, was this seat taken?' he said, rather sharply, knowing it wasn't.

'No. It's... Fine.' She glanced at the few empty seats dotted around the place, the seats he should have taken, away from her and everyone else.

With her mug empty, this seemed as good a time as any for her to grab her coat and leave. Although, she had no idea where she could go. She couldn't afford to use the heating in her flat and somewhere with warmth would be ideal. The thought of the many shops on Princes Street occurred to her. She could slowly browse through each rack while keeping warm, but then she would come across things she desperately needed but couldn't afford; like boots without holes, and gloves without holes and everything that she owned but without holes; she was beginning to feel a bit like Swiss cheese.

She thought that maybe she could take a plunge back into the overdraft that she had just paid off. She definitely *could* do that. She argued with herself internally over the matter as she began to put her soggy coat back on.

'I wouldn't be so keen to leave.' the man advised, still appearing to read his paper, 'It's a blizzard out there.'

She looked out the window and saw exactly that. Snowflakes were smashing themselves up against the glass in a hysterical flurry. The sight of it summoned goosebumps from her skin. She begrudgingly put down her coat and eased back into her seat, although it felt uncomfortable now. She had no issue sitting opposite a stranger while the unwritten rule of ignoring one another remained unbroken.

Unfortunately, he had spoken to her, breaking that sacred rule that a private person like Haidee depended on. If she continued to overlook him, she would be rude and antisocial. She had no other choice, there was only one thing to be done now: small talk.

'You been to the Christmas Market?' she asked, diverting her eyes to everywhere he wasn't.

He didn't respond. She drummed her fingers on the seat, wondering if she should ask again louder or just brave the blizzard.

He raised his eyes over his paper to look at her, 'Sorry, was that a question for me?'

'Yeah.'

He let his newspaper fall into his lap and took a sip of his coffee before answering, 'I have been to the Christmas Market.'

She nodded and he stared, expecting her to ping pong the conversation back to him. Her plan to relieve the awkward tension began to unravel. His eyes stayed fixed on her without a single blink.

'I haven't had the chance yet.' she said quickly, 'Not this year, I mean. I grew up here, used to go all the time, but it's changed a lot now. Not that it's bad, just different.'
'It has changed, a fair bit. I've been in the city a *very* long time.' He had a very smug smile, which made Haidee curious, 'So why haven't you been this year?'

She shrugged, 'I'm waiting to go with friends.'

'Surely you can have a wee nosey on your own?'

Haidee shook her head. The thought of going in there alone made her heart wobble, 'It was... I used to go all the time with my mum. Doesn't feel right alone.'

The man put his coffee down and looked very sympathetic towards her, 'I'm so sorry. How did you lose her?'

'What makes you think I lost her?'

'The way you said it.' He smiled softly, 'It's clearly a tough topic.'

She nodded, 'Just plain old bad luck, I guess. The doctor's couldn't give us a real reason. She was healthy and young. It was a heart attack, but that didn't make sense. They said it might be stress...'

'You don't seem convinced.'

'The only thing she had to stress over was me and by that time... I was really ill, really really ill and then suddenly I was better. And then she died. It just... Doesn't seem right.'

Haidee then became aware of the personal information she was divulging, and the fact she was handing it out to a stranger more readily than she handed out her leaflets. Embarrassment, accompanied by a small amount of anxiety, forced her mouth shut, but the stranger continued the conversation.

'That is bizarre. I'm really sorry. I know what it's like to lose someone close to you. A time of togetherness can remind you of what you've lost.'

She hummed a confirmation, refusing to let another detail slip from her lips. There was something about that man, he was suspiciously easy to talk to.

'I'm sure your mum was a lovely woman.' he said, as if he possibly could have known.

They were just kind words, empty kind words, from a stranger probably feeling as awkward as she did now. In that moment, she thought it was impossible to come up with a more uncomfortable conversation.

'Do you ever feel like someone is watching you?' The man proved her wrong.

She giggled nervously, scolding herself for attempting to socialise and wishing, for once, that she was outside amongst the arctic weather, 'Well, you are, right now.'
'We're having a conversation. What I mean is: someone you haven't noticed is watching you.'

There was a knot in her stomach. That feeling had been constant and yes, she had that feeling as they were speaking. She had assumed the sense had lingered from the old woman looking at her earlier. The fact he, a stranger, would say something like that made her feel naked, defenseless, vulnerable. It was odd that he took the chair opposite her, out of all the empty seats available. An unnerving theory began to web itself in her mind, connecting events that seemed completely unrelated. She speculated that he sat there on purpose, and that he could have even followed her in there. Maybe, just maybe, he was on Princes Street the night that she almost got hit by a car.

He pointed over his shoulder, her eyes darted on command to a young boy. He looked no older than sixteen and had an intense stare on her. He jolted up in his seat and with a face glowing red, snapped his head back to look at the wall.

She laughed to herself then looked back to the man who now had a smile on his face, 'How'd you know he was staring at me?'

'I saw him while I was in the queue, I'd say he's been staring for at least fifteen minutes.'

'Well, I guess that's flattering in a creepy way.'

'I wouldn't feel flattered. It would be one thing if he smiled back, but pretending he wasn't watching you means he never wanted you to know. *Very* creepy.' The man took another sip of his coffee, all the while staring at her, which she found to be worse than the boy watching her, 'Sorry, am *I* creeping you out?'
'Yup.' She tried to keep a polite tone, 'Not the best topic for small talk.'

'Would you rather talk about the weather?' He gestured to the whirling whiteness outside.

'I don't even want to think about the weather.'

He nodded in agreement, 'I was only trying to make the point that we doubt ourselves too much. Trust your instincts. Have a little *faith* in yourself.'

She grinned at the absurd route the conversation was taking but felt free to speak absurdity back, 'But I get that nagging feeling when I'm alone in my room. So, obviously, it's just a feeling.'

'Obviously, there is someone in the room.' He shrugged innocently.

Perhaps it was from the draught that trespassed into the cafe the moment someone opened the door, but she blamed his eerie manner for the sudden resurfacing of her goosebumps.

She tried to wipe them away with the warmth of her palms and said half-jokingly, 'You really like being creepy.'

'Well, I do like to talk about creepy subject matters. I'll tell you though, you shouldn't be scared if you get that nagging feeling. If you say you know you're being watched, the watcher will give themselves away.'

'But the watcher is the reason I'd be scared.'

'If you don't face your fear it will never go away.' he chimed, moving a black coil of hair behind his ear and turning his focus back on his newspaper, 'It'll keep on watching.'

Now that the conversation had swerved off a social cliff, it was definitely time to go. She left him without a goodbye, though he didn't seem to care, and took refuge in a toilet cubicle for the next hour and a half, for warmth's sake.

CHAPTER 4
GABRIEL'S MESSAGE

Contact.

Warm fingertips grazed against Haidee's palm as the woman slipped the leaflet from her hand.

Connection.

Eyes locked, a soft smile that gave acknowledgement to Haidee's existence.

Appreciation.

The smile opened, letting out a soft and delicate voice, 'Thank you, this looks great.'

The woman blended back into the crowd. That was the most interaction Haidee had with a human that day, or any creature for that matter. She did attempt to pet a dog, but it rushed by her to mark its territory on a phone box and never looked back.

Despite the swiftness of the moment, the kind gesture made her feel like a person again, warming her heart and defending it against the ice-cold exteriors of others. Sadly, it did nothing to defend her against the actual cold.

The weather wasn't as bad as it had been the last few days; the wind blew occasionally as if to quietly remind you that it was still around; the grey sky had no intention to rain on anyone's parade, just to dull it, which only made the abundance of fairy lights appear more effective; and the cold only nipped at Haidee's nose, turning it as red as a certain famous reindeer's.

Today might have just been bearable, if a ghost of Christmas Past hadn't turned up.

'Hey- Deeeee.' he sang, in a broken raspy voice that scratched like sandpaper against her eardrum.

Filled with dread, she turned around slowly, looking for the ill-begotten face that matched the voice, but she failed to recognise anyone. She began to worry for her mental health; paranoia that someone was watching her, and now hearing voices. Great.

'Lang time nae see, Dee.' She saw a pair of lips move, and was gobsmacked at the face they were attached to.

Pete, for as long as Haidee knew him, which was seven years- give or take- had always looked as shit as his personality. A shaved head, revealing his pale and spotty scalp, with veins throbbing up through his forehead. Bloodshot eyes, from sleepless party nights that flew by in a haze thanks to prescriptions he swiped from his gran, or somebody else. Cheek bones, finger bones and ribs, hollowed out by the pill-based diet. Baggy decade-old clothes that hung on him like rags, reeking of fags and frayed at each thread. This was not the Pete who stood before her now.

This Pete could almost pass as handsome. His clothes were smart and neat, not strangers to the washing machine or an iron. He was still slim-built but had full rosy cheeks and strong-looking hands. His eyes were those of someone who knew a decent night's sleep, and his rich brown hair waved across the tip of his ears, reminding her of Leah's natural hair.

'Ye look surprised.' He smirked.

She wouldn't be fooled by his makeover, that smirk was a classic Pete-the-Prick smirk.

'Why are you here?' She got straight to the point.

'Christmas shopping, ain't ev'rybody?'

'No. Some of us are working to earn our money, you know?'

'Aye. Got maself one of those wee job *things* tae. Thought I'd see whit aw the fuss wis about.' He muffled a laugh at his own sarcasm.

'Oh really? Back to being a salesman? Going door to door? Selling, let me guess, hash? Eccies? Crack?'
'I'm a repairman.'

Haidee's laughter slapped the smirk right off his face, 'The universe works in mysterious ways.'

'Whit dae ye mean by that?'

'Well, considering how skilled you are in breaking things. Does Leah know you're in town?'

'Aye, well, better be. I'm crashing at hers.'

Confusion, disappointment and rage melded into one sickening emotion. Pete could read this from her face and took delight in what he saw.

'She's ma sister, no yours.'

'Are you sure about that?' she grumbled, 'What kind of brother mugs his own sister?'

She was hoping to wipe the smile off his face a second time, but apathy had glued it on, 'Families fall out an' make up aw the time. Ye'd ken that if ye had one.' He began to walk past her, 'I'll probably see ya around.'

Haidee turned on her heel and grabbed his arm. 'You better have changed more than your appearance.'

He nudged her hand away, 'Aye, I have. I'm daeing a lot better, looks like I'm daeing better than ye tae.'

He looked her up and down, almost wanting to lick his lips at how deliciously the tables had turned. She was the sickly-looking, poorly-dressed, desperate one now and she knew it. The fact that Pete, of all people, could take a victory in that devastated her- but there was no time for self-pity- that nagging feeling had returned.

She quickly looked over her shoulder, but as always, there was nobody watching.

'Whit's got intae ye?' Pete laughed and began to walk backwards, 'Cannae even face me now?'

The creek of metal drew both of their attention above, turning Haidee around to get a better look. An angel decoration, the same size as her, smiled softly down on her. Its arms seemed to stretch wider and wider, until she realised it was toppling over the edge of the building.

Haidee jumped back, stumbling into Pete as the angel shattered into a thousand pieces on the spot where she was standing. The shards scurried between their feet, some flying into the air, scratching at their clothes. There were some gasps, a few curse words and a screaming child, but Haidee just stared in shock as she fell flat on her arse.

Pete laughed hysterically, clapping and walking away, 'Yer face wis priceless, Dee!'
A group of older women helped her to her feet as the owner of the shop came out and looked at the damage, apologising profusely and assuring everyone that the angel decoration did pass the safety regulations.

'That was lucky,' one of the women said, 'Are you alright, hen?'

No. It wasn't lucky. No. Haidee was far from alright. She was a rationalist down to the bone. An Atheist, a realist, she worshipped science and documented evidence was her bible. But now, she was in doubt. Two near-death experiences within a week, plus the constant feeling she was being watched, it all felt too much of a coincidence to truly be a coincidence at all.

CHAPTER 5

It Came Upon A Midnight Clear

Every word Ms. Fraiser spoke glided on a disdainful sigh, 'We do not tolerate skivers.' Haidee struggled to tolerate hypocrites, yet she did her best not to mention how her employer had three tabs up on her monitor; Amazon, Youtube and an article on home remedies for wrinkles. 'We need people here who are committed to promoting our clients.'

'I nearly got hit by a Christmas decoration!' Haidee began to plead, 'I was too... shaken up to work the rest of my shift- I understand not getting paid those hours, but please! It's Christmas, and I need this job!'

'Haidee, don't exaggerate. I heard about the angel incident, and you're clearly unharmed. And don't act like it's the first time you've gone AWOL during a shift, we do keep an eye on our staff.'

The truth had cornered Haidee. She couldn't deny the umpteen breaks she would take for shelter and regain warmth, naively thinking that she wasn't being spied on. No wonder she was feeling constantly watched.

'That's your employment with us at an end, I'm afraid.' she gave a little apathetic shrug, and continued with her online shopping, while Haidee quickly fled before the Ice Queen could see her cry.

And cry she did.

The tears blinded her as she tried to dodge the rush of holiday shoppers, causing her to knock shoulders and incur their wrath. Swears and insults followed after her as she desperately tried to think of a place she could hide for a moment, for a breath, for a second to herself. A fruitless effort; thoughts rotted in her brain, spoiled by the panic alarm shrieking in her mind, alerting her of BILLS- BILLS- BILLS- to pay for her refrigerator of a flat.

The overwhelming responsibilities weighed her down until she couldn't move. If that wasn't enough, the feeling of being watched was growing stronger and stronger. The crowd rushed around her like rapids against a rock, pushing against her- but still she couldn't move. Faces flew past her, many eyes staring and glaring as they passed. Then, through all the pushing, there was a pull. A hand locked onto hers and guided her through the stream of people.

As they made it to a small arched close, she rubbed away her tears to reveal her blurry saviour.

'What happened?' Leah asked. Concern had tamed her loud and proud self momentarily, into someone gentler, adapting to her friend's fragile state.

'I-I-don't- I lost- my job- and- I don't-' Haidee had abandoned the calm and balanced demeanor Leah was used to seeing. It was as though they were two completely different people; they had never met this side of each other, but the bond was too strong for them to ever feel like strangers.

Leah pulled her into an embrace, a protective shell where Haidee felt able to cry out all her built-up stress and devastation. After the last tear had fallen, Leah took her back to her flat, a lazy den of half-done chores and organised mess. Once there, the friends dug into a plate of microwaved chicken korma whilst sitting on the couch, but Haidee was so grateful, it almost tasted as if it could be home-cooked.

After a few quiet chews, Leah spoke words she had been holding back for the last week, 'Matt told me about yer flat... I ken yer proud, Dee, but let us help ye! Yer jus' goin' through a shitty time- we aw have shitty times, but you been there through mine. I'm gonna be here through yours, yer gonna live with me, awright?'

Haidee was ready to argue, but the sight of Leah's worried expression weakened her heart further. She couldn't save face when it was covered in tears and she couldn't keep her pride when all she felt was disappointment in herself.

After a moment of silence she finally admitted, 'I don't want to be a burden.'

'Ah, ye'll be nae bother.' Leah patted Haidee's ankle, the closest thing she could reach, 'Honestly, I could use the company... I've been meaning tae tell ye...'

'Pete's back.'

Leah looked surprised, 'Aye. How'd ye ken?'
Haidee told her about their unfortunate meeting and the incident that came after it and Leah reacted animatedly to each sentence; frowning, laughing and gasping.

'He says he's daeing better now, and he looks it.'

'He definitely looks different, but I don't want you getting hurt again.'

Leah stared off for a moment, then shrugged, 'He's ma brother. I love him no matter how big ay fanny he is.' She put down her now finished plate and cuddled into Haidee, 'And the same goes fer ye.'

'You calling me a fanny?'

'Aye. Only fannies dinnae bloody ask fer help!' She grabbed her hand, 'Stay. My casa is yer casa. Save some money, get back on yer feet.'

Haidee gave a very slow, very painful, nod, 'But I need to go tonight.'

'Why?' Leah lamented.

'Well I need my stuff, my clothes- my knickers especially.'

'Just borrow mine!'

'No,' Haidee giggled, 'I am trying to swallow my pride, but you need to let me wear my own knickers, and use my own toothbrush!'

'Oh, that's ay point. Love ye and aw, but I'm no ay minger!' She pondered for a moment, then headed to the kitchen and began pulling out various packaged biscuits and crisps from the cupboards, 'Ye go hame. Ye pack. Ye eat. Yer back here in the morn'. Got that?'

Haidee nodded, not acknowledging that Leah's back was still turned.

'Got that?'

'Yeah, I'll be here.'

'Alright then,' she handed a carrier bag full of nibbles to her, 'I'll see ye taemorrow morn', flatmate. If I dinnae, I'll march right up tae that igloo ye call hame, knock doon yer door and drag ya here!'

Haidee beamed at her friend through watery eyes, feeling both pathetically helpless and incredibly thankful. A bittersweet cocktail to digest.

Plodding along Princes Street, writing a list in her head of things to do, Haidee began to feel the weight leave her shoulders. However, her mind immediately construed Leah's kind support as another debt to pay, one that Haidee didn't know how to repay.

St. John's Church marked the meeting of Princes Street and Lothian Road, looming over those who populated the night, some already staggering from a little too much mulled wine. Headlights danced across its windows, pulling Haidee's attention away from her thoughts and to her left, an open gate and the entrance to St. Cuthbert's Cemetery. After the day she had, she'd much rather have a quiet stroll amongst the dead than deal with the living.

It was eerily alluring the moment she walked down the steps. Small shards of light from the streets and windows poorly lit the hallowed grounds, just enough to make out shapes from the shadows. A turquoise bust of a man sat within the wall. Years of rain had made its mark on his cheeks like streams of tears; his eyes followed her as she passed, but she was relieved to not feel as if it were watching her. That feeling had been absent since Leah had found her. The more she thought about it, the more she convinced herself her paranoid feeling was just a side effect of the stress.

She continued around the manor, strolling by the marked graves. Age had worn away most epitaphs, leaving ghostly words that haunted those who walked by with the suggestion that everyone is eventually forgotten. Some of the larger slabs had fallen and smashed over their graves, giving an ominous sense of unrest to even the most grounded of people; as if the dead were now disturbed. Contradictory to most people's feelings, graveyards acted as a sanctuary for Haidee, especially at night. It was a place of rest, after all.

She could see the buses and crowds as she approached the steps. She could hear music blaring through a car window amongst the wheezing and heaving sounds of engines. She could smell kebabs, cigarette smoke and wet newspaper. People passed the gates at the top of the stairs; a young girl with headphones, a large man with shopping bags and a couple that were attached by hips and mouths.

Her role had become a spy in the shadows, a spectator, a specter, protected by a gate that stood between her and the lively streets of Edinburgh. She wondered how nobody could notice her staring. They were too preoccupied with their own lives to be aware that she stood just at the bottom of the steps. If they had lost focus for just a moment, if they had let themselves soak in their feelings and instincts, they might have felt her eyes on them.
Just like Haidee felt eyes on her, once again.

The emotional day had blurred her senses, until now, and she became strongly conscious that the feeling of someone watching had never really left her at all. She knew she wasn't the only spy in these shadows.

The heavy sensation pulled her gaze over her shoulder. She could see Edinburgh Castle, sitting tall on its rocky hill, its walls made into a fiery gold by the show lights.

She could see the silhouettes of gravestones, still and lifeless amongst the moss and trees. She could not see anyone looking at her. She could not see anyone at all.

Yet, that feeling held her with an unyielding grip. She looked around again- at the manor house; nobody at the windows- under the arched shelter beside the steps; sleeping bags and newspapers. Clearly there had been someone there but not now. She was completely alone.

She tried to move on, up the steps, towards signs of life but the feeling dragged her back amongst the dead. In a determination to relinquish the sensation, her mind offered up the conversation that she had with that strange man, nearly a week ago, and the suggestion he gave.

"If you say you know you're being watched, the watcher will give themselves away."

'I know you're there.' Each word tumbled into the air as mist from her mouth, 'I know you're watching me.'
Expecting this little experiment, this small piece of superstition, to prove that it was just her imagination, she looked once more, convinced she'd see exactly that. Nothing.

But there he was.

His glare tore right through her, through every fragment of logic and every shard of rationality that was holding her together.

There he was: sitting on a gravestone, one foot against its faded face and one foot in the grave.

There he was: a grey sallow face half hidden by shadows.

There he was: with branches of light stretching from his back like solid lightning bolts that danced in the air, completely and utterly out of the realms of nature.

And there *she* was- bolting up the steps.

Back on the crowded streets of Edinburgh, she pushed past each individual, not waiting for the lights to give her permission to cross the road, then nearly being hit, again, for it.

She kept running, despite the raging honks of horns and dodged each obstacle, each baby in a buggy, each dog on a leash- not stopping- never stopping, until she was back in her flat; her top floor igloo.

She tried to switch the light on but it refused. Her pay-as-you-go meter was empty. She cried into the darkness, stumbling to her room where her blankets and duvets and rugs and towels were waiting to give her any warmth they possibly could. She kicked her wet boots off her feet and dove right in, pulling all she could over her, as if it would protect her from the apparition she had witnessed.

She told herself she imagined it. She told herself it was all the weed she'd had over the years. She told herself she was ill and it was causing her to hallucinate. She told herself it was for being hungry for so long, then she told herself it was what she ate. Every and any excuse she could think of, as irrational as it may be, she would tell herself in a feeble attempt to convince herself that what she saw she didn't see at all. No matter how desperately she tried, she could never succeed while that feeling still lingered: the heaviness of his stare.

The feeling was with her now. As if he were standing in the corner of her room. She needed to know he wasn't in the corner of her room. She needed to know it was all in her head. Despite the fragility of her screaming nerves, despite the quivering of her heart, she had to move the edge of her duvet down her face and peer over.

There he was.

CHAPTER 6
Mistletoe and Jager Bombs

In a dizzy kaleidoscope of moments, struggling to pull apart what was happening from what had just happened, Haidee came to the conclusion that she was completely and utterly plastered. Leaning against a wall, which she had mistaken for the floor, she attempted to figure out the wheres, whats and whys of her present situation.

It was a battle just to move. She could feel her arms and legs being nibbled by a pins-and-needles sensation. When she finally did make a single step, her world seemed absent of gravity, and although she saw both her feet on the ground, she could feel her consciousness floating away. Sensibility had always prevented her from getting this atomically drunk and regardless of her senseless abandon on this occasion, she vowed to never repeat this mistake. Whether she would remember that vow was a different matter.

This was a part of Edinburgh she hadn't been to. The buildings around her held all the enigma of past centuries with their columns and paned windows, yet they lacked the wear of time entirely. Pinks and blues and greens shined above her head, stretching from roof to roof over the wide street: a cobbled plaza with empty benches. A distant sound, muffled under the ground, vibrating through her; a familiar old Christmas anthem, with the steaming Scottish youth chanting along.

The party was beneath her feet. As she turned to walk down the spiralling stairwell and join the merriment, a snowflake floated by her. Then another one. Then a few. Then more and more, until it could be confidently said that it was snowing. Through her numbness, her heart latched onto this instant, perfectly preserving the moment in her memory, like a snow globe she could shake up at any time. While she didn't know where she was or why she was there, she felt happy. That was all she needed to know.

Underground: the music danced with her intoxication and took her mind for a spin. Face after face flashed by only to be instantly forgotten, until one of the faces was already remembered.

'You're a healthy colour.' A sarcastic note from Matthew, who was holding a pint in each hand. As always, both were for himself; a solution for an avid drinker whose greatest obstacle was getting to the bar. He went on to ask her about the music and pulled out a fun fact or two, but each word bounced off her weak concentration. She nodded when given the cue to do so by his facial expressions, but she found herself enjoying the feeling of dipping her head and continued to do it consistently.

Matthew laughed, 'You alright?'

She waved his question away from her, 'I. Am. Good.'

'Yeah?'

'Yes. I. Am. Good.' she spoke each word carefully, in an attempt to sound sober, but only succeeded in sounding like a computer-generated voice.

'Cool, I'll get you a drink of water.' he said, unconvinced and handed her his two drinks, 'You're gonna be in this spot when I get back.' And off he went, to bravely barge through the wall of drunks, thirsty to enhance their intoxication.

She stared curiously at both glasses, watching the stream of golden bubbles hurry to the foam. Each glass was moist with the dew of a newly poured pint but neither felt wet. Neither felt cold. Neither felt heavy. A spontaneous tremble took control away from her hands. For fear of dropping them, she placed the drinks on the dance floor and took a seat on the frosted glass flooring.

She pulled at her top. Bright blue sequins shimmered like rippling water as she tugged at the fabric. It was a top she'd seen many times, craved each time she thought about it and couldn't remember ever buying. Nor could she recall having enough pennies in her bank to do so.

The music shifted from the jingle jangles of nostalgic festive tunes to the bass thumping new-day beats that were guaranteed to fill a dance floor. In that instant, colours blazed beneath her. A whole rainbow and more flashed their way from one corner of the room to the other.

Cautiously, she pushed herself up, feeling the beat pulse through her, the only feeling her nerves would register. A sudden energy sparked within her, thoughts began to take form in movement. A sway, a swerve, a shuffle building into twists and twirls of every limb. Dance had taken root in every bone.

She swam through the mass of movers and shakers, being swept into the current of the rhythmic language of their bodies. The adrenaline was rapid. She jumped up and down, reaching the surface for gasps of air, waving her arms excitedly as she allowed herself to drown in capering bliss.

Familiar fingers laced through hers, tugging at her knuckles and pulling her to face Leah who was also delightfully drunk. They grinned empathically, no words needed to express their elation. They pushed their heads together as if to better connect their minds and echo their joy through telepathy. With a slight effort, they swayed to a song that played in their minds, slower and much different to the one in their ears.

Matthew reappeared, reunited with his two pints and holding a glass of water in the bend of his arm.

'Lucky they survived!' he shouted over the music, nodding to his much-beloved alcohol.

The girls giggled as Haidee reached for the water, 'I think I need this.'

'Agreed.'

She began to drink as Leah lay her sleepy head on Haidee's shoulder. However, the more Haidee drank, the more thirsty she felt. The floor lights began to flash faster, her dizziness forced out an awkward laugh, as she did not know what else to do. Anxiety crashed through her enjoyment, bringing paranoia with it. Instincts pulled her gaze in one direction- the flash exposed the sallow face of a man, a familiar face that evoked terror, then the next flash spirited him away along with that feeling. The tremble returned. She pulled the glass from her lips and tightened her grip, worried that the drink would slip.

Instead, it shattered. The flashing stopped. The shards rained from her fist and some of them stabbed her palm. Blood dripped over the webs between her fingers and down both sides of her wrist. This was a cue for the sharp shooting sensation of pain. The throbbing. The piercing. All were a no-show.

The kaleidoscope had returned, twisting her moments faster and dizzier than before. Leah's shock. Matthew getting help. The glass being taken from her hand. In the street: Leah waving down a taxi. Backseat: pressing someone's scarf to her palm. Leah asking, 'Are ye no in agony?' Matthew saying, 'I think she's in shock.'

Automatic doors. A receptionist looking concerned. A&E waiting room. A boy staring at her from his stretcher as they passed. Leah rubbing her back. A nurse bringing her to a room. Watching the tweezers pull small bits of glass from the gashes. Edinburgh Castle in the distance, surrounded by stars with morning breaking to the left. Trying to eat chips from a polystyrene box with a dressing on her hand. Leah holding the other hand.

It was late in the afternoon when Haidee woke up. She stroked the dressing, pressing lightly on her wounds that were definitely aching now. She was safely cocooned in the warmth of her duvet, in her well-heated bedroom, in the flat she had shared with Leah for the last three months.

The unusual amount of alcohol that had entered her system caused her temporary amnesia, forgetting her home, her job and her bank account that currently had eight hundred and seventy two pounds and sixty three pence. Although the hangover applied a haze on everything, she could vaguely remember the past three months, although it was more like remembering a dream.

She had moved in with Leah, found a job as a waitress for a very swanky restaurant and was currently living her happily-ever-after. The fridge was full of good-quality fresh food; she had new clothes in her wardrobe and not one of them had a single hole; she had no problem paying rent, which was a lot more affordable than when she was living on her own and she had no debt whatsoever. She could even afford luxury toilet paper. Her life was a fairytale come true.

'How's yer hand?' Leah asked from the doorway to Haidee's room.

Haidee turned over in her bed and smiled, 'Clumsy.'

'Ya think?' She was holding two mugs of tea and put them both on Haidee's bedside table.

Leah then sat next to her, sprawling her legs out on the bed and taking Haidee's hand to inspect.

'Ye'll live.'

'I wasn't in any doubt of that.' Haidee chortled and took her hand back, feeling the ache spread to her fingertips, 'I've survived worse.'

CHAPTER 7
It's The Most Wonderful Time Of The Year

Entering the kitchen, she had forgotten what she had gone in for.

Haidee looked from the kitchen porter, who was charging through with bags of brussel sprouts, to the chefs who sliced and diced and mashed and stirred in unison. The steam from the pots and pans spiralled up to the ceiling, filling the air with the scents of leek and potato soup, fried onions, roast parsnips, turkey, pigs in blankets and much, much more. It smelt like Christmas.

Registering a name to a face, with a helpful nudge from his nametag, Armin the kitchen porter put a tray in the serving queue and shot her a quick smile, 'Table 18.'

She lifted the trey very gingerly, afraid that the four cocktail glasses, each on their own individual decorative china plates, would crash to the floor. They contained shredded lettuce leaves drizzled in a rose-coloured tiger sauce, coated with a dash of spice, adorned with a slice of lemon twisted elegantly in the centre and featuring about two dozen prawns arranged in a perfect circle. Even if they didn't slide off the tray, a slight flinch or twitch and the beautifully mouth-watering arrangements would be less than perfection. Her stomach agreed that this would be a terrible shame.

Impressing herself, she managed to escort each starter to their destination safely, bringing delight to two formally-dressed middle-aged couples. One of them complimented her shoes, a flattery which she took graciously. The shoes *were* absolutely amazing. A perfect balance of aesthetic appeal, comfort and affordability, which she had never found in footwear before. In the past, there seemed to be an unwritten rule where if it looked good, it felt terrible; if it looked terrible, it felt good; and if it looked good and felt good, you'd have to take out a mortgage in order to buy them.

Another of the four pointed out the bandage on her hand and asked after her wellbeing, questioning whether she should be working. She minimized the story of the glass incident to sheer clumsiness, then assured them that she was more than capable of working and enjoyed doing so.

The Maple wasn't just a restaurant but a temple of appetizing ambience. With its vine-covered walls, glistening chandeliers and vintage dining sets, this was the first choice for question popping, milestone reaching and every celebratory moment. With curiously vague menu choices like the Kelpie Supper and Royal Pallette, if people were unsure what they had actually ordered, they were at the very least sure it would be lusciously extravagant. This was a place for making people feel special and as a member of staff, for the first time in any job, Haidee did feel special.

Busy, busy, busy. Order after order came in. Her hands and feet knew exactly what they were doing, where to go and what to take, while her mind struggled to keep up. The mad rush left her memory to grasp at certain moments, taking a mental picture of customers' faces, only to forget them the minute they walked out.

She finished at seven o'clock, just before several table reservations were about to be filled. She waved goodbye to her envious coworkers as she walked out the door guilt-free. After eight hours of serving for other people's celebrations, it was time for a little celebration of her own.

'IT'S CHRISTMAS!' yelled through the speakers over the ice rink, the popular Wizzard song came to an end, fading into the next Christmas jingle.

Leah's laughter was contagious as she and Haidee failed to keep a graceful balance, slipping and sliding in their rental skates. Matthew skated ahead, showing off by racing backwards. Their friends Dom and Yana went at their own cautious pace, clinging onto the side walls in fear of ending up like Leah, who had fallen flat on her arse in a hysterical giggle fit.

Next: the big wheel. Cosy in a carriage, they tried to calm the nervous Dom down as he expressed his fear of heights and his, irreversible, fatal mistake of joining them. Yet, by the time they reached the top his tune had changed. They all took in the breathtaking view of Edinburgh. The Walter Scott Monument brooded amidst the festivities, the castle was lit up in red and greens and Princes Street radiated with sparkling lights. The gardens filled with all the attractions glowed, Waverley Station was busy with its trains coming and going, and Calton Hill was sitting quietly in the distance. They could see everything. As amazing as the view was, he still chose to skip out on the star flyer.

An inextinguishable grin appeared on Haidee's face as her feet dangled in the air as the suspended chairs were lifted 60 metres above the ground. She watched Yana scream in excitement beside her, Leah's blonde hair whipping in the wind and Matthew watching the world go by contently. Despite the unnatural distance between her feet and the floor, she felt exhilarated as she flew through the air; like a comet dazzling around the world. She smiled down at Dom, who would not be able to see that she was doing so, wondering how he could miss out on such an experience because of something as silly as fear. As she passed the monument an umpteenth time, a strange sense tugged at her mind.

She turned her head to look at the monument's arched window but the ride was already spinning downwards. The strange sensation whispered a little thought, a little notion that someone had been watching her, but she brushed the feeling off, immediately. Of course there were *many* people watching the ride.

The group dispersed on seperate quests and reunited on a garden bench once each of them had been victorious. Yana brought five hot toddies; Dom brought five paper plates full of bratkartoffeln; Leah brought three bratwurst hotdogs; Matthew brought two angus beef burgers and Haidee brought ten mistletoe kisses to share. Dinner was served.

By the time they had gobbled down their food and had bursts of flavours excite their taste buds, small white flakes had begun to float down from the sky. The flakes clung to Haidee's blue coat and nestled on the ground, turning it white very quickly.

'It's snowing!' Yana pointed out the obvious, her childlike glee warming the hearts of her friends.

'Christmas isn't far behind.' Dom grinned, 'Better get wrapping.'

'Shit! I need to go shopping.' Haidee cringed, disorganised as ever.

'We've got plenty ay time.' Leah grinned back, 'Dinnae worry yerself.'

She wasn't worried, far from it. She had never been so at ease in her life, sitting with her friends, bellies full, watching the snow fall around them. This was everything she wanted for her life: simple happiness. Counting the days seemed unimportant; all that mattered was here and now.

But there was something out of place.

The drink in her hand did not feel warm. The air around her did not feel cold. She watched a snowflake float down past her eyes and onto the back of her hand, where it melted into a small droplet. There was no feeling to it. No cold, no wet.

As Leah and herself walked past stalls, admiring all the crafts and trinkets, Haidee had an overwhelming notion that there was something that she was forgetting. It was an intense worry, certain that this slip of the mind could have grave consequences. The thought had slid through the cracks of her consciousness, just out of reach. The stove was definitely off, she checked that with Leah. Her wallet was safe in her handbag and she clutched her phone inside her pocket. Her keys were in there too. All that she was responsible for was secure. But there was something. A shape was taking form in her head. It wasn't a something at all, it was a someone.

'I'm having the time ay ma life!' Leah said, warping the shape in her head and preventing a revelation, 'Aren't ye?'

Haidee smiled as if to say she agreed and to avoid telling a fib. It should have been the time of her life. Confusion scratched at her brain as she looked at each stall. She couldn't understand why she felt uneasy staring at chocolate in the shape of tools, or glittery crochet scarfs, or dried fruit decorations. A small voice within her cried that it was all wrong.

The nagging feeling had returned, pulling her head around to where she felt a stare. For a brief moment, a picture formed in her head of what she was certain she was about to see. A click, a light switch, a bolt of lightning, this is what she *needed* to remember, but the image erased itself and any memory of it before her eyes reached the spot. She tried desperately to think the image back into her mind but the harder she thought, the further the idea slipped. Whatever it had been, she didn't believe it was in front of her now.

Leah tugged at her hand but it took a moment for her to realise she had done so. She stared down at their hands linked together, wondering why she couldn't feel the softness of Leah's gloves, 'Yer daeing loads better than before.' A wild grin spread across Leah's face, 'Aren't ye happier than ye've ever been?'

Haidee questioned if she really did feel happy, when it seemed as though she may feel nothing at all.

CHAPTER 8

I Wish It Could Be Christmas Everyday

'Everything appears fine.'

Three words that were meant to be positive, that were meant to give relief, but only brought hopelessness. There is a big difference between appearing fine and being fine, and Haidee was anything but fine. A vast amount of nothingness had replaced all feelings, with the exception of frustration, confusion and upset.

'Then... I need more tests.' She told Dr. Chowdhury, who was still looking through the information on her computer, 'I can't feel anything, so there's gotta be something causing it?'

She turned to give Haidee her full attention. Her tone was very soft and sympathetic, but her expression was that of a stern school teacher, ready to tell off their disobedient pupil, 'It is not to say that what you're experiencing isn't real, but I believe your symptoms are all psychological. It could be brought on by stress- it is a very stressful time of year-'

'I'm not stressed!' Haidee snapped, instantly realising how her demeanor seemed to contradict what she had just said, 'I mean, *this* is stressful. Not getting an answer, not knowing what's wrong, this is what's stressing me out.'

'I am giving you an answer, Haidee.' Dr. Chowdhury continued, calmly but more serious than before, 'It might not be the answer you want, especially because it doesn't have an easy fix, but from what you are telling me, and what the tests are showing me, is that you are dealing with an issue that is psychological. Now, what I'm going to do is refer you on to a psychologist, they will be able to get to the root of your problem and give you the treatment that you need.'

'How long is that going to take?'

'It will be after New Year's until anything is sorted- in the meantime...' She hurriedly went through her filing drawer, banging and clattering, making the delicate Haidee wince, 'You can have a look at these.'

She handed Haidee several leaflets, all to do with mental health and services she could call, with images of people getting support from a nurse or a doctor, something she felt was a tad ironic in that moment.

Dr. Chowdhury picked up on her irritation, 'Haidee, I'm sorry I can't do more for you at this time, and I understand it's frustrating, but the psychologist will be able to help you. Until then, I recommend spending a lot of time with friends and family, doing what you enjoy- just focus on the positive.'

'This isn't in my head.' Haidee began to weep, 'There's something really wrong, I know there is- I don't care what your tests say- I'd rather be sick right now. I'd rather be in pain than feel nothing.'

'A lot of my patients would say the opposite.' Dr. Chowdhury did not look impressed but the feeling was mutual.

Haidee didn't truly wish for pain or illness, only for the numbness that had possessed her body to be exorcised. It had been harder to endure than any ache, sharpness or throbbing she'd ever experienced. While she was certain that it wasn't in her head, it was certainly making her lose her mind.

She carried trays to tables as though they were weightless. Every step she made was accompanied by the thought that her foot may never return to the ground, followed by surprise each time she watched it do so. The tremble would return at the most inconvenient of times, causing her to smash a glass in the middle of The Maple.

All eyes were on her as she swept the glass. Whispers and mutters created an unnerving dissonance, as if the customers came from a world where accidents never happen. Control was slipping through her fingers and she anxiously awaited the day that she would let go completely. Her very existence had become something fragile. The sight of blood alerted her that she had cut her finger. It didn't matter. Nothing felt as though it mattered.

In between work and her arrival at The King's Theatre, there was a blank space that her memory failed to fill. A swarm of people squeezed themselves through the doors of the century-old building; Haidee, Leah and Matthew began to shuffle themselves into the gaps in the crowd. However, the people moved around them, forming a path which they could walk with ease, without even acknowledging the three of them. This delightful convenience was not an experience Haidee could believe was happening. Adding to the suspicion was how quickly and easily they reached their seats.

Then, through her numbness, she could actually feel something. A sensation which she had felt many times before, itching the back of her neck, telling her that there were eyes on her. She tried to reason with herself as she looked around to see if anyone was actually looking. She would catch the eyes of people who happened to glance in her direction and, in doing so, she eventually became the one who was staring.

Matthew turned to her, 'I hope you're gonna watch the stage when the show's on, get your money's worth.'

She giggled because she knew it was her cue to do so. Another feeling she had lost was familiarity. While she knew that she knew Matthew and Leah, her ability to recognise them had been disabled. The seat she was in felt uncomfortable, not due to the lack of legroom for her numb unfeeling limbs, but due to the sense of being trapped in between perfect strangers.

As the narrator's voice boomed throughout the lavishly-detailed auditorium, colourful lights danced on the rising curtain, then fell onto the stage. A cheesy parody number played and the adult dancers impressed with their precisely-timed leaps and twirls, while the child dancers brought glee with their adorableness. Then, the dame was introduced, tickling children's funny bones with silly voices and faces whilst throwing several innuendos over their heads for the adults to catch. The pantomime had begun.

While people laughed and cheered, Haidee sunk in her seat, wishing for it to end. The jokes were logically humourous but she had no laughter to give. The musical numbers were successfully entertaining everyone else, but she could barely keep focused. She looked to Matthew when he booed the villain of the pantomime as loudly and lively as possible. She watched Leah when she was laughing so hard that she almost choked on a chocolate raisin. It was clear that Haidee was the only person in the room who wasn't in the moment.

Her eyes climbed from the stage up to the ceiling. It was decorated with a mesmerising image: a woman donning a robe of stars who reached out towards the moon as a shadowy figure crawled after her through the clouds, offering the sun up in his hands. The clouds swirled around them and carried the iconic masks of theater, the faces of comedy and tragedy.

'He's behind you!' everybody yelled the quintessential phrase, trying to get Goldilocks to turn around before it was too late, but she pretended to have an IQ of a snail and looked in every other direction, as is tradition.

In that moment, the audience's warning resonated with Haidee. She could feel it, the stare that burned into the back of her neck as though it were the painted shadow creature that was crawling after her, with his offering of the sun singeing her senses, causing her to feel the stare and only the stare.

'He's behind you!' they shouted again and she instinctively whipped her head around to look behind her, her focus landing on the exact spot that she felt the stare came from.

There was nothing and no one. For the briefest moment, she thought she may have seen something but her mind had instantly erased it. Her mind dug through the last few moments, trying to snatch back the memory that was slipping until her mind caught one image: a place.

She could picture it vividly: the gravestones with their faded words, the bare trees with their branches slicing through the street lamps' light, the crying turquoise bust in the wall, the parish church and a chilling view of Edinburgh Castle. It was St. Cuthbert Cemetery.

Leah tugged her attention back to the stage while her mind remained on the image of the graveyard. While the show went on, her thoughts disinterred every memory associated with that place, but her mental exhumation provided no new findings. Nothing of consequence ever happened there, not that she could remember.

But she knew: there was something that she was forgetting, buried away in her subconscious, with only a faint idea to mark that it ever existed.

After the show ended, and they exited the building as easily as they entered, Haidee looked to the clear sky and wondered about the last time she saw rain. Of all the weathers, rain was the only one she couldn't stand, which was her tragic irony of being born scottish. However, her mind craved it, now that she realised it had been missing for so long. The last time she could remember feeling raindrops on her skin, she was still handing out flyers.

'Oi, Whit's the matter wi' ye?' Leah playfully slapped her on the back, 'Panto no yer cup o' tea?'

Haidee examined Leah, noticing the more she focused the less she looked like Leah.

'Aren't ye happy Dee?'

'I don't know.' She said quietly, becoming uncomfortable around the woman she had been friends with since college.

'Really? Whit's wrong?'

'I don't know.' She said louder this time, feeling the words swerve from her mouth as she lost control of her emotions.

Leah tried to comfort Haidee by placing a hand on her shoulder; a hand she couldn't feel, attached to a person she no longer recognised. She could start to feel something: dread.

Haidee tried to jog her memory, knowing that it must have rained since she had been flyering- this was Scotland- clear skies and dry ground throughout winter had to be one sign of the apocalypse. She could remember snow- which she couldn't feel- but not a single raindrop since she had been fired from that job four months ago.

Four months ago.

All feelings had returned, crashing through the walls of her physical apathy. A ball of pain twisted and screwed through her stomach, making her feel as though she was about to vomit. She was shaking. Shock cracked the foundations of her reality, the laws of physics crumbled. The conclusion terrified her: none of this could possibly be real.

'How long is it until Christmas?' She asked pleadingly to Leah and Matthew who simply shrugged off her question.

'Long enough.' Matthew said, 'You've still got time to get our presents, if that's what you're worried abou-'

'No!' she barked, 'No- what day is it?'

'Dee, ye need tae lie down.' Leah stroked her arm, 'Especially if ye cannae even remember whit day ay the week it is.'

'What's the date?'

Leah rolled her eyes but Haidee persisted.

'Leah! What's the date you asked me to move in?'

'Do you really want to go back to that life?' Leah said. Her smile didn't flinch, 'This is a wonderful life, wouldn't you rather stay here than go back to being cold, hungry and miserable?'

Haidee's eyes widened. It started to dawn on her that the numbness she had been suffering from was something she had encountered many times before. It was the surreal detachment of dreaming.

'29th of November.' she said faintly, afraid that her words may break the world around her, 'That was the day you asked me to move in and that was four months ago.' She watched as Leah's and Matthew's smiles melted away, 'How can it be nearly Christmas if it's meant to be March?'

Silence befell Edinburgh. The scenery around them desaturated and dimmed. In an instant: all the cars, all the people and even all the birds had been plucked out from the world. All that remained was Haidee and the two people disguised as her friends.

'Haidee, don't fight it.' Not-Leah spoke with a voice too soft and light to be her own, 'You have a brilliant life here.'

'Where the fuck is here?'

'A better place.'

'No!' she shrieked, her mind too weak to suppress the furious anguish that was burning inside her, 'This is hell! I can't feel anything- this isn't real- you're not real! Who the fuck are-'

The memory smashed into the front of her mind. That nagging feeling, that stare, it belonged to a man. The man who had appeared out of thin air in the graveyard that night. His sallow face and the branches of light that surrounded him, she now remembered vividly; it felt impossible that she could ever forget.

She ran, as she had done that day. As pointless as she knew it was, there was nothing left to do but run. She was scared of what she did not know, and yet, she was scared to know it. She could remember it all clearly now, shivering under the duvet in fear, peering over the edge- that man- that creature, had found his way into her room. He flew at her, the dark pit in the centre of his palm blindfolded her. He had caught her and had somehow transported her to a place where nothing was real. In her mind there was only one conclusion for her to come to, but she was not ready.

Ready or not, the truth was coming. The unreal Edinburgh had bent and warped beneath her feet, changing the entire map of the city, swirling and morphing until she was back in that graveyard. There was no safety in this situation. She couldn't turn back, she couldn't turn it off, she was in this ghastly circumstance of impossibility and there was no escaping it.

As she made her way down the sloped pavement into the cemetery, the feeling of being watched grew heavier. The parish church that lay in the middle had a light glowing from the windows that caressed the edges of every tombstone. She peered into the windows, scared to see if someone was staring back but desperately needing to know if there was, to know where her watcher was.

There was nobody. The stares seemed to pull at her from another direction but just as she turned to look, he spoke.

'This is no ay scary place ye know.' his voice bellowed, causing her to jump out her skin and whip her head to where her ear had guided it.

She saw no one. There wasn't anybody there. It was just the wall with plaques and lamps hanging from it. Then, she noticed it.

'It's really quite ay bonnie place, even fer the living.' said the turquoise busk of William Bonnar from his hovel in the wall.

Haidee slowly lowered herself onto the ground, unable to do anything but stare in bewilderment at the talking likeness of the dead man.

'Oh dinnae be so wide-eyed, lass!' he snarled, 'At the very least, I should be entertaining, am I no?'

'I think I understand now,' Haidee nodded to herself, 'I've smoked too much, this is just a really bad trip and I'll wake up and be fine.'

'This can all stop if ye want it to. Just go back hame and dinnae say another word about it.'

Surrealism had lunged back onto her nerves, making her feel distant enough from what was happening so that she could manage to speak calmly enough to the dead man's busk, 'I have no home here.'

'Af course ye dae, go back and talk tae Leah, ye'll feel much better there than here in ay graveyard with ay bunch af dead folk, eh?'

She shook her head, 'None of this is real. I just want real- I want reality.'

'What's fun about reality, ye can have anything ye want here! Name it and ye'll have it!'

'I don't understand where here is!' Haidee cried out, trying to deny the suspicion that was itching at the back of her mind, 'I don't understand what is happening!' She felt that stare heavy on her back, 'I don't understand!'

And then one thing came back to her: the words of that creepy man in the coffee shop.

She got up to her feet and turned her back to William Bonnar, looking towards the rest of the seemingly-empty graveyard, 'I know you're there. I know you're watching me and I know you're there!'

And there he was.

A familiar stranger. This time, he was not surrounded by lightning but his grey eyes struck fear in her just as intensely as a single bolt. His stare had its own touch, like a hand that grabbed Haidee by the throat, making each word spoken and breath taken a struggle. Determination demanded she push through.

Terrified to know, but unable to go on without knowing, she had to ask, 'Who are you?'

He didn't speak.

'Why are you following me?'

He stayed silent.

'What do you want from me?'

Not a word.

Tears rolled down her face. She was so unsure of everything but his existence. He was real. The rest of the world wasn't. Not the path beneath her feet, not a single brick in the walls around her, not even William

Bonnar who had spoken to her a moment ago. It was just her and her Watcher.

Anger cultivated inside her. She hadn't been able to feel anything in so long, and fear dominated all other emotion, but she wouldn't let it. She was fighting it, replacing it with rage and resentment. There was nothing he could do to her that he couldn't have done four months ago. She wouldn't let him scare her.

'Spit it out! I deserve to know what the fuck is happening to me!' She charged at him but he backed away.

He stopped when she stopped, leaving the distance between them just as it had been.

'Why won't you tell me who you are?' She looked him up and down, trying to find some indication of who he might be.

He appeared to be no different than any other man she would pass on the street: a slightly haggard young man in a tattered jumper. His face suggested only a few years between them but his eyes told another story: one far too long to tell.

'Are you dead?' she asked as, considering all that was happening, this seemed like a logical guess.
'Not quite.' he finally spoke, his voice soft and light, not what she had expected at all.

'So you're alive?'

He shook his head. Looking directly into his eyes, she stepped a little closer towards him. This time, he stayed rooted in place, but he was clearly uneasy in doing so. He was determined to keep eye contact with her but the glimmering tearfulness of her eyes forced him to turn his head, as if ashamed.

'No.' he said.

'Then what?'

He watched her from the corner of his eye. She was much closer now, more than she intended to be. Both of them felt uncomfortable yet both were resolved to stand their ground.

He turned his head to face her directly, and with an airy breath, he said, 'I am Death.'

There was a brief absence of thought and emotion inside Haidee. His voice lingered around her, waiting to be contemplated. Eventually, she allowed herself to understand his meaning and what this meant for her, the very thing she concluded moments ago. The logical reaction, as she knew it, would be to cry hysterically and mourn for herself. However, nothing about this situation was logical and neither was the laugh that escaped her.

'What, so you're like the Grim Reaper or something?'

'Or something, yes.' He was slightly insulted by the sudden elevation in mood.

'You look like you shop at Next.' She smiled while tugging at his jumper, 'Do you get special discount there?'

'Are you taking the mince?'

'Well...' She rolled her eyes, feeling a lot more relaxed, 'One minute I think I'm going crazy, then I know I have 'cause some guy is telling me he's the Grim Reaper, wearing a pretty cosy-looking jumper.' She shrugged, 'Honestly, at this point, fuck it. I think I've been such an emotional wreck recently that I'm finally past the point of caring. Okay, you're the Grim Reaper, I was talking to a stone head in the wall a minute ago. I'm just going to roll with this.'

The gape from his mouth indicated that he was more shocked at her reaction than she was at his confession.

'I don't think you understand me.' There was almost a growl in his voice, 'I am the influence of Death. A messenger, if you will. I have one purpose. I move lives from this world to the next. I think your question of what I want with you is clear from who I am.'

She became very still, imitating the many gravestones around her. Her amused state became a temporary blockade between her and the truth.

She nodded very calmly, 'So *I am* dead.' finally speaking her suspicion out loud.

He didn't speak.

'Did I get sick?' With watery eyes, she gazed up at him, 'I was sick wasn't I? I should've used the heating, I should've done better at my job- Or did the job make me sick?'

'You weren't sick.'

Her lip quivered, 'Well I'd like to know how I went. Is Leah okay?'

'Leah's fine.'

'What about my dad- I hadn't seen him in ages.'

'He's fine.'

'I mean they know I'm dead right?'

Silence, again.

'Oh God, am I still in the flat?' She began to bubble into another hysteria of tears, 'Shit! Am I just rotting away in that flat?' Her legs began to wobble and balance abandoned her.

Quickly, he grabbed her arms to aid her balance. She shuddered, feeling his warm hands on her skin, realising how cold she actually was. A gasp escaped her as she savoured the feeling of another person's touch. A bittersweet joy to indulge in. There was a relief in feeling something real again. Unfortunately, it had to be him, the one thing in this nightmare that she wished to be imaginary.

The feeling of her icy skin was a strange feeling to him as well, and she could read this on his face.

'You're fine.' he assured her, but this was met with a blank expression.

'Explain. Explain everything.' she pleaded, 'I'm so confused right now.'

He obliged, 'You're not dead... but you should be.' She heard him but still didn't understand, 'You were meant to die when you were wee. When you were really sick, remember? The doctors didn't figure it out in time. Pneumonia, that's what you had.'

'But... If I was meant to die, then why didn't I?'

'I honestly can't tell you. I don't know, but you were living off borrowed time and now that time is up.' He stroked her shoulders in an attempt to offer some comfort, 'I made this world in your head, filled it with everything you wanted, I wanted you to die happily. It only unravelled because you fought it the entire time. You wouldn't let yourself be happy, even in your ideal life.'

'Well that's a miserable thought- that a basic and normal life was my ideal one.'

'It's easy to appreciate the simple things when you go through hard times. I can fill this world with anything you want. This is just what you yearned for.'

'Couldn't you have filled it with... pet dragons, if you could fill it with anything?' she joked, wiping the tears from her eyes, 'I love dragons.'

'Name it, I'll do it.' He grinned excitedly, 'I can make anything you want!'

'You can't make it real, though. You can't give me the real Leah...' Her heart ached for the warmth of her friend's hug, 'I can't feel anything here. I can't taste all the wonderful food you made here. I can't smell it anymore, I can't feel my friends hugging me.' She began to cry again, 'No, I don't want any of this. I want reality.'

There was sympathy in his eyes, she could see it there. Nevertheless, he had a purpose and it had to be fulfilled, 'Haidee you need to come with me. You need to let me pass you on. You're not meant to be here.'

Her head shook his words away in a refusal to listen but they clung to her, echoing until they were heard. The realisation was as crisp as ice. She was aghast, and it had only just occurred to him what he had just foolishly given away.

'I have a choice in this, don't I?' she laughed, hope igniting in her veins, 'You can't kill me without me letting you, otherwise I would be dead!'

'I don't want to kill you.' he said firmly, 'This isn't killing, you are *meant* to be dead-'

'You want to take my life- that'd be killing.'

His grip tightened around her arms, 'This is my job, my purpose. I pass on people who need to be passed on. You're meant to be dead, Haidee.'

She pushed him away, harder than she had intended. The branches of light reappeared, striking the darkness from his back, flickering in and out of visibility as he stumbled backwards, 'No! Fuck this! Fuck you! You put me in a fake world against my will, tell me it's for the best 'cause I'm meant to die- but I have a choice in this. I'm not dying, I won't go with you!'

'Haidee McLean, your time is up. This isn't a choice. Your life is a defiance against nature. You cannot fight it!'

'I can. You said it. This world unravelled because I fought it the entire time.' She glared at him, frustrated that there was any moment where she had seen him as a person, when his intentions made him a cold-blooded killer. A monster. She wouldn't just agree to be murdered, 'I clearly have a choice in this and I choose life.'

The darkness began to creep and crawl on the walls behind him. His grimace held terror for her, but she refused to look away. He charged towards her- she considered running but assured herself that he could not hurt her or he would have done so already.

The shadows grumbled, and it did so loudly; he had to shout, 'You can steal more time but not enough to escape this! Dying isn't the worst thing in the world,

Haidee, are you sure you want to run from me?' He extended his hand out to hers.

The darkness had devoured the fake world whole. It was just the two of them now, in the middle of a black canvas. The grumbling had stopped and silence had fallen upon them.

'I'm sure.'

Those words pierced through him. He closed his eyes, looking somewhat in pain and then opened them again to stare directly into her soul, 'Then enjoy what time you have left. You can't escape fate.'

With a flicker of the lightning from his back, he slipped out of sight. Cracks broke their way up through the darkness, harsh light broke into the void, along with noise and the warmth she'd been sorely missing. The canvas around her tore apart and she felt as though she was falling through the air. All the sweet memories she had of that pseudo-world happened simultaneously around her. She fell past fireworks, engulfing her in sparks of gold, ruby and emerald; she fell past Edinburgh Castle and the Christmas Market, all rolling and breaking apart above her; her flat and Leah vanished out of sight; the amazing restaurant that she worked at whizzed past, it's chandeliers spinning like fiery tornados; everything shot past her as she felt herself fall back into reality.

Her fingertips could feel something soft beneath them. Her head nestled into the plumpness of a pillow. The smell of disinfectant, orange juice and mint chocolates overwhelmed her nose. She could hear talking in the distance. She tried to open her eyes but was immediately blinded by the light.

A familiar voice announced to the world that she was awake.

CHAPTER 9
O Come All Ye Faithful

Light spilled through the stained glass windows, planting a colourful garden of translucent flowers on the grey stone floor. Lit depictions of saints and disciples looked gracefully upon the people in the High Kirk: some there in prayer, others in curiosity. Footsteps treaded carefully around the echo and voices were hushed in respect.

There was one person, however, who strode around the church as if it were his domain: a man with a black mesh for hair who dressed in attire so formal it outdid those in their Sunday best. This gentleman spoke loud and freely, speaking to a woman in one of the pews. What he said was encouraging, supportive and positive, and as he spoke it was visible that the weight of the world was leaving her shoulders. Yet, she stared through the gentleman, and every other person in the church took no notice of him- except one.

The Gentleman looked over his shoulder to see The Watcher, doing what he did best. The Gentleman gave a smug smile, then continued talking to the woman. The Watcher, with a sour face and an impatient manner, began to approach the man, each step more determined than the last, until he was right behind him.

'You know it's rude to interrupt.' The Gentleman hissed through his grin, rising from the bench and tilting his chin upwards as if to raise himself to The Watcher's height.

'I think we're both beyond manners.' The Watcher said sternly, looking about St. Giles' Cathedral, with the sensation that even the bricks in the walls did not welcome him, 'I need to chew your ear off about something, I'm guessing you know what.'

The Gentleman gestured to a pew and they sat down together, 'Just promise me your owner won't whistle you back at any moment. I can't have you reeking of death in here.'

'He knows I'm visiting you.' The Watcher reassured, 'This is a priority.'

'Auch, really? I feel well special!' The Gentleman slapped one of his cheeks, pretending to blush, 'I've never been death's priority before! What an honour.'

The Watcher made sure every muscle in his face expressed the bitterness he was feeling, 'Why is your signature on Haidee McLean?'

'Wouldn't you like to know?'

'Aye. That's why I'm asking.' he said, bemused by the gentleman's attitude, 'She's on my list, you know I can't cross her off when you've marked her.'

'Weel... that does sound like a problem, fer you.'

'Right, well, don't tell me why. Just take it off of her so I can do my job.'

The Gentleman feigned to ponder for a moment, turning his head this way and that, squinting his eyes at the prospect, before returning to his animated demeanor, 'Nah. I don't think I want to do that.'

'For Christ's sake! Why no?'

'Do not take His Lord's name in vain.' he said pedantically, 'Especially, not in His own house!'

'Am I supposed to believe you care? None of this lot can hear us anyway.' He gestured to everyone else in the cathedral, who were oblivious to their presence.

'You'd be surprised what they can sense.'

'I'm sensing you being a pain in my arse.' The desperation began to seep through in trembles and twitches, 'You're in my way, at least have the decency to explain why?'

The Gentleman leaned back in his seat observing the holy medieval building and the beautiful craftsmanship detailing this refuge for believers. There was an abundance of Christmas decorations, with more Christ than commercialism, but barely a change from the ones that decorated the church last year. He was far too familiar with every decoration, every painting, every statue and tapestry in all the holy temples in Edinburgh.

'I'm so lonely.' he finally said.

Disbelief raised one of The Watcher's brows to its highest capability, 'So you did this for attention?'

'No. I did it long ago as a favour, and kept it on as a grudge.' he decided to speak freely, 'I remember Haidee vividly. Wild wee bairn, very energetic- until the pneumonia. The doctors misdiagnosed it as just another bug going about; it would have killed her if I hadn't put my signature on her. I saved her life.'

'What are you playing at? Fuck sake! You're talking like you're some hero- you know you're not supposed to intervene with death!'

'And your lot weren't supposed to intervene with faith.' he retorted, 'I spent over a century, alone, looking for a successor and I found one. All I had to do was save her child and she'd have absolute faith.'

'You're talking shite. Where is this successor of yours then?'

A sinister grin spread across the gentleman's face. 'Do you not remember? Haidee McLean was the child that Arthur wouldn't take.'

Shock struck so hard that years vanished from The Watcher's face, revealing a confused and sad little boy. It was a long time since he had heard Arthur's name and just as long since he had allowed himself to think about his old friend.

'There was a debt due and it had to be paid.' The Gentleman shrugged, staring blankly into the distance, 'Death collected.'

'Then why is this happening now?' The Watcher asked, 'If the debt had been paid, why is she on the list now?'

The Gentleman shrugged and opened his arms as if to the heavens, 'Everything we do is for a reason. That girl must need to be dead, now, for a reason.'

'Then you're going to erase your signature?'

The smugness that radiated from the gentleman alerted The Watcher of his decision before he even said, 'Of course not.'

The Watcher pushed himself up from his seat and stormed away from the other side of the pew.

'Oh, don't go away in a huff!'

'Your signature can't protect her if I can convince her to die.' he called back, charging towards the exit. 'If I have to torture her, so be it!'

'Wait, wait, wait!' The Gentleman called, lunging over the back of the pew.

His words lassoed The Watcher, bringing him to a halt. A instant sigh of relief escaped from The Watcher's lungs, believing The Gentleman had seen sense and would prevent him from having to do something barbaric. He turned back around.

'Just out of curiosity, how did you know it was my signature?' The Gentleman's mischievous smile forced the dread back onto him, 'Why not, say someone like, Hope's?'

He was reluctant to speak, not wanting to give The Gentleman any gratification, but felt he could make one last effort to reason with him. 'When I realised that somebody had intervened and that's why I couldn't take her, I gave her a fantasy. Everything she wanted. She rejected it. She couldn't even feel it. The only way that was possible was if she had complete faith in herself, in her instincts.' A sudden jog of his memory encouraged his anger, 'I sent a car to hit her- it wouldn't have killed her with your signature on her- do you know how much shite we'd be in if she bled out and was still breathing? Did you not even consider how much pain she could suffer if anything, that would usually be fatal, happened to her?'

'Don't get your knickers in a twist. I gave her friend a nudge to be in the right place at the right time.'

The Watcher's eyes grew narrow as he realised his acquaintance had been one step ahead the entire time, 'You bastard. You spoke to her, didn't you? She called me out because you suggested it.'

'Yes, well, people do listen to my advice.' The Gentleman sang triumphantly, 'And you're not the only one watching Haidee McLean.'

With one foul scowl, The Watcher left the cathedral without another word. A few of those in prayer shuddered. Death and Faith always had a wavering relationship. In some moments they were great allies. In moments like this, they were bitter rivals, a circumstance nobody would wish to get in the middle of. Unfortunately, someone already was.

CHAPTER 10
No Small Wonder

Leah was inconsolable, rambling on through bubbling moans that made it impossible to decipher what she was saying. She just managed to get the point across; she was glad Haidee was alive.

Haidee's father stood at the bottom of the bed, deep in thought and it was not a pleasant one. The doctor stood awkwardly in the room unsure what to say.

'All the tests came back clear.' She nodded reassuringly, 'You are perfectly healthy, absolutely nothing to worry about.'

This was familiar news that once angered Haidee. However, she felt certain this was the truth; just as she was feeling itchy from the bedding, full from the meal she just had and happy from just being able to feel again.

'She wouldn't be in hospital if she was perfectly healthy, would she?' Haidee's dad scowled at the doctor, 'Nobody goes unconscious for five days for no bloody reason, ay?'

'She wasn't the fittest when she came in.' the doctor began scraping together a vague theory, but it was clear from her wavering voice that she was unconfident with her attempted explanation, 'She was borderline malnourished and exposed to cold temperatures. Sometimes... The body reacts strangely to certain conditions. She does have a history of illness. I'm sorry we don't have a satisfactory diagnosis. The main thing is that she is healthy now- but we will expect you, Miss McLean, to go to your GP for regular checkups, just to keep an eye on things.'

Her dad rolled his eyes. The doctor gave a polite nod to Haidee and left the room. Leah grabbed onto her hand and continued to wail at her, while her dad continued to huff and puff in the corner.

'I feel fine.' Haidee tried to reassure them, 'I think a good sleep was what I needed.'

Her untimely joke only provoked more tears from Leah and more worried looks from her dad.

'We'll get you home and take care of you.' he said, 'Moira makes a good casserole. On her meals, there'll be none of this malnourished crap happening.'

'I'm going to stay with Leah.' Haidee said weakly. Leah nodded, attempting to smile at Haidee's dad but failed to look anything other than miserable.

'She can't look after herself, let alone you.' he grumbled, 'We're family, come home.'

'I'll be better now that I'm with Leah.' Haidee insisted, 'And she's a great friend, she'd have taken care of me sooner if I'd let her.'

Leah nodded, ululating a tangle of words directed at Mr. McLean which left him less than convinced.

'No, Haidee, you're coming home with me. You need to be looked after properly.'

'Dad, I'm twenty-six.'

'And unemployed and malnourished- in the freezing cold winter!'

'And getting help and support from the doctors and my friends. I make my own decisions, I'm staying in Edinburgh.'

'Stubborn- I don't know where you get that from, your mum wasn't like that at all!'

'But you are.' She grabbed his hand and squeezed it tight. 'I know you'll never stop pressuring me to come home, and you know I'll never say yes.'

'Is it 'cause of Moira? I know yous have never really got the chance to... bond, but you get on well.'

'It's not 'cause of Moira. It's 'cause I want to be living my life, in my city, with my friends.' She smiled softly hoping he'd understand.

It was a reluctant sigh of defeat, but it loosely translated to his acceptance of his daughter's choice. Haidee then grinned towards Leah, the real Leah, in all her emotional state. She felt tired, nauseous and achy, and glad of it. Every single nerve-tingling sensation was welcome, good or bad.

The hospital discharged her that day and Leah welcomed her back to her tip of a flat. Haidee had remembered it being pristine, organised and decorated with bright furnishings within that makeshift Edinburgh she'd been trapped in. In reality, there were crumbs on the floor, dirty dishes everywhere and a dodgy smell that could only have come from the week-old pizza that had been laid to rest in the bin. Apart from random bits of tinsel thrown about and the faux ficus with an angel sat on it, the place was hardly decorated. It was far from perfect but she immediately loved it for all its flaws.

Leah's flat was only one bedroom in reality. However, while Haidee was in her dreamland, her friend had bought a futon mattress just for her and decorated a corner of her bedroom with voiles over a clothes horse to add a touch of privacy; a gesture that warmed her heart.

They stayed up most of the night, talking about what had happened during the days she had missed; not months as she had dreamt. Matthew had visited just about every lunchtime, he'd brought After Eights for her but Leah, being a nervous eater, had devoured all of them. She promised to buy her a new box but Haidee didn't mind; she found the story amusing. Yana, who they hadn't actually seen in months and was no longer with Dom, had visited and left her a card signed by herself and some other friends she had made through volunteering at the Fringe Festival, many years ago. Leah had met up with her brother for lunch, which he surprisingly treated her to, and even more unlike him, he comforted Leah and accompanied her to the hospital a few times.

Eventually tiredness weighed them down and the usually-chatty Leah couldn't string a sentence together. Haidee tried to sleep on her futon beneath the veil of voiles but she was not permitted to. Fear was keeping her hostage. She was afraid what would happen if she was to fall back asleep. She was afraid she'd never wake up again.

It didn't matter how much she tried to reason with herself, she could not convince her anxious mind that all she had experienced was a dream. Logically, every ounce of it had to be fake: from her life of perfection to The Watcher in the graveyard. She desperately tried to refuse to believe in him. She wanted to refuse to believe in that nagging feeling that pulled at her, telling her that he was in the room, even now. A little residue of craziness: an aftermath of a five-day coma.

Sadly, living in a fake world for what felt like almost half a year opened her senses to what was truly real and what was not. Without a doubt, she knew the truth of this situation. The Watcher was real and he was watching her right now.

CHAPTER 11

Little Saint Pete

Despite being unconscious for five days, Haidee would have been happy to sleep through another day, really sleep. No dreams. No fantasies. What she wanted was for her mind to take a break in a black void, take a break from all the thoughts and worries, just for a day. However, her mind had been fractured and, through the cracks, notions of death crawled into her forming dreams, infecting them until they deformed into horrific nightmares; starring her Watcher and his sallow face. Sleep was impossible, and the fear was draining the life from her.

Never before had she looked so ill. The warmth of her complexion had been chalked over, dehydration had cracked her lips and her eyes looked bruised from exhaustion.

'You look like death.' Leah placed a reassuring hand on her shoulder, as Haidee glared at her through the compact mirror, 'You were out fer five days, a course yer gonna look shite.'

'Thanks.' Haidee made a pathetic attempt at a laugh.

Leah was up, energetic, fully clothed and ready for work. In contrast was Haidee: sitting on the futon, exhausted, in her dressing gown and ready for another slow day of unemployment. Leah didn't invest in wi-fi, only data, preventing her from using the most convenient method to hunt for a job. While she did have a few printed CVs ready to hand out, her body wasn't ready to endure the bitter Scottish weather. Her coat was waterproof, but thin, and she still had the issues of her clothes seeming as though they had been tortured by a hole punch.

'You can borrow ma jumper,' Leah offered, nodding to her wardrobe, 'Yana's coming 'round later. Matty's working, but she said she'll pop in.'

Leah left for work and Haidee spent the day trying to distract herself from her thoughts. She and her dad texted, he was still adamant that she should move back with him but accepted that it wasn't what she wanted.

Most of her day was filled with animated films that reminded her of her childhood, welling up her eyes with tears of nostalgia. She ate a lot of soup and a lot of toast and drank an excessive amount of herbal tea. Yana visited, made awkward small talk and left after an hour. It was clear she was uncomfortable, as she always was when something bad happened, but she tried her best to uplift Haidee's spirits.. Haidee was grateful, both to see the real Yana and for her considerate nature.

Still, dread had stayed with her despite all her attempts to ignore the feeling. Fear held her captive in the flat. She stared out of the window looking for The Watcher's grim face in the outside world but it didn't matter how much she didn't want to know it, she did know that she wasn't alone in her captivity.

'You'd be really bad at hide'n'seek.' she tried to say lightly but the tremble in her voice gave her away, 'It's pretty easy to find you. You're a literal pain in my neck.'

Heavy shoes muffled thuds against the carpet. Fabric scuffed against each other, and the springs of the couch moaned tiredly under weight. She began to pivot herself steadily. Her heart struggled in her chest; all she wanted to do was run but the door was closer to him than it was to her. She'd have to face him either way.

Her vision staggered across the walls, reluctant to find him. Her fear begged her not to look but her stubbornness and determination were in control now. She had to face this.

There he was- *Pete.*

She cursed in surprise, stumbling backwards, grabbing onto the window sill to steady herself, 'What the hell are *you* doing here?'

'Why the hell ye acting surprised?' He raised a brow, 'Thought I wis ay literal pain in yer neck?'

'Not you- I thought you were…' she trailed off, bewildered. A sudden wave of relief washed over her. Maybe it was all a dream, maybe that nagging feeling was just paranoia after all. She began to laugh, further confusing Pete.

'Thought I was who? Leah? Is that how you talk to her, eh? Some friend you are.'

Haidee picked up a cushion from the armchair and launched it towards him, smacking him in the face.

'Watch my pus!'

'Why are you here? Leah's at work.'

He pointed the cushion at her, in as threatening a manner as he could with a cushion, 'Oi, that's no way to treat someone who's doing something nice for you.'

'Giving me a heart attack? How thoughtful. You practically snuck in, I didn't hear you at all- hold the phone…' She glanced suspiciously between him and the door, 'That was locked.'

He looked unamused, 'Aye, and?' She stared him down for an answer, 'I have keys. Leah gave me ay spare.'

Haidee remained unconvinced, feeling that entrusting Pete with access to her home was even too naively generous for Leah.

'I've changed.' Pete quickly tried to win her over, witnessing the suspicion in her demeanor, 'Honest, I have. I had ay couple, well, several rough years- that I made rougher fer the people 'round me. I ken that, I ken.' His eyes dropped guiltily to the floor, 'Ye've been ay guid friend tae Leah and I thought ye might no wanna be on yer own.'

Haidee didn't know what to make of him. The lines between reality and fantasy were still blurred for her. While her conscious mind was beginning to slowly accept that The Watcher really wasn't real, because obviously he couldn't be, deep down she was certain he was. It wasn't an ideal time for her to judge anyone's character.

'I've binged just about all of Leah's Don Bluth and Disney DVDs...' She headed towards the kitchen, 'Do you wanna put on something, I'll make tea.'

'Aye, but it wilnae be ay chick flick.' He chortled looking through the slanted stack on the shelves.

Rolling her eyes, Haidee put on the kettle. Pete started criticising the majority of Leah's movie collection but his words were, thankfully, being drowned out by the rumble of the kettle. She allowed her mind to drift, focusing on the rumble. Pete was staring expectantly at her, or so she thought, until she turned to see that he was still looking through the stack and prattling on. She shook her head but couldn't shake the feeling.

As the click of the kettle cued the cease of the rumbling, she poured the tea and was about to venture back to the seating area, but her peripheral vision made the startling discovery.

Both mugs crashed to the floor, smashing all over the wood. The scalding liquid spat over her socks, burning the skin of her feet. She yelped, steadying herself against the couch, hurriedly yanking off her socks and wiping the freshly-brewed tea off her skin.

'Jeezo!' Pete yelled, leaping towards Haidee, 'Whit the hell happened?'

Seeing that Haidee was trembling, he tried to comfort her by gently patting her shoulders, but she shrugged his hands off, feeling patronised.

'I'm fine.' She snapped, 'Just put a movie on, I'll fix this.'

'I dinnae trust ye with any mare boiling hot water.' He grabbed a towel and began to clean up the mess, 'Ye pick the movie, I'll make the tea.'

She nodded begrudgingly, and began to examine Leah's collection. Pete whistled as he tidied and prepared two new cups of tea. She took a deep breath and looked over to Leah's room, the door slightly ajar. He wasn't there now, but she swore that she saw The Watcher again.

'I smoke weed every now and then.' she said, catching Pete's full attention, 'Is it normal to hallucinate afterwards? Have you had that? Or heard of anyone who has?'

He laughed, 'No unless it's been laced wi' some guid shit. Did some pink elephants give ye ay fright there?' His expression changed when he saw she wasn't laughing along, 'I hallucinate, and get delusions and aw that- obviously, I've taken harder stuff, and it does mess wi' the head over time... It's aw neurological, eh? It's like ma brain's constantly been triggered to basically... dream while I'm awake, so it just does it on its own sometimes. I suppose being in a coma for a wee bit will do the same- but it's probably just temporary for you!' He held his hands up, quick to try and reassure her, 'Like I said, I've taken hard stuff, and y'ken I've been doing that fer ages.'

She smiled and gave a short nod. While she was a tad surprised that she was taking advice from Pete of all people, it was the exact reassurance she needed. She had been in a coma for five days, dreaming of another world. What she saw wasn't real, just a normal side effect.

The Watcher wasn't real. He wasn't real. *He's not real.*

CHAPTER 12
Do You Hear What I Hear?

Haidee clung to the collar of Leah's jumper, which she was borrowing. It was a thick knit and plum coloured, Leah's favourite colour, and it smelled just like her; a combination of flowery Ted Baker body spray and cigarettes.

She felt if she clung to the woolly jumper beneath her jacket, not only would she feel a tiny bit warmer walking the streets of Edinburgh, but she would feel less alone. It had barely left five o'clock and the sun had already abandoned the sky, leaving the amber light of street lamps to warn off the darkness. Still, the presence of shadows on the outskirts of the path were enough to make Haidee feel uneasy.

The day had been a busy one, walking from store to store handing out as many CV's as she possibly could, which was a pitiful amount. The vast majority of her time was taken up by irked members of staff explaining to her that she should have handed in her CV at the beginning of November, that they had just hired their Christmas staff and wouldn't be looking to hire again anytime soon.

Haidee knew her chances of finding a job at this time of year were slim, but she was determined to find one. There was only one alternative option, and even the idea of it grappled at her stomach, squeezing it tightly: Universal Credit.

Every single person in her life had suggested it, even Pete, and Leah insisted she do so, that it would help her get back on her feet. Matthew had told her to get over her pride, that she deserved every little bit of help that she could have. It was too depressing a thought to share with her friends, but the issue was no longer pride, it was guilt.

She was slowly accepting that all her coma dream had entailed was straight from her imagination, and what she had experienced in the lead up to her collapse was paranoia and hallucinations brought on by her deteriorating health. Yet, there were thoughts and feelings given to her in that dream that she couldn't shake off. The strongest one, the most miserable thought of all, was that she wasn't meant to be here, and if she was to take money from Universal Credit, she'd be taking someone else's place.

As she dwelled on her miserable thought, the feeling of a stare upon her returned. It stayed with her, like a spotlight, making her visible even as she walked into the dimmer and darker areas of Edinburgh.

She started humming a Christmas tune to herself, one of the classics, Mariah Carey's *All I Want For Christmas*. It was a silly attempt to try and lift her spirits, one that failed as she began to think of all she actually wanted for Christmas. A job, a home, health and financial security. A great contrast to what she wanted as a child, and a sure sign that she was now, indeed, an adult.

Her mind summoned up a memory to comfort her. She remembered the smell of cranberry filling the room from the dozens of scented candles scattered about. The tree stood in front of the window, showing off the decorations to all the neighbours; handcrafted that year by her, her mother and her grandmother. A silver angel sat on top of the tree, looking down at the presents that lay beneath it; boxes and lumpy shapes covered in shiny gold, red and tartan wrapping paper.

That was the last Christmas with her mother.

The image of her mum was stuck on one version, the way she had looked in the framed photo currently by Haidee's futon. She had dark curly hair like Haidee's, a huge red lipstick grin, thin 90's-esque eyebrows and a peach-coloured tank top. The photo was taken in summer, but there she was in her memory of Christmas Day, wearing that same peach tank top.

Haidee recalled getting a lot of clothes and socks that year, each time she thanked her parents with an obliging smile. There may have been a few Playstation games, and a Polly Pocket set. She wasn't entirely sure, but that could have been the year she got her first handbag; a turquoise one with an illustration of Ariel from The Little Mermaid.

While she quite liked everything, she remembered hiding the disappointment of not getting the one thing she really desperately wanted, the only thing on her Christmas list that year. She had written several letters to Santa begging for it. All she wanted was a puppy.

What she got was a cuddly toy dog and a card explaining that puppies are for life, not for Christmas. A phrase that confused her at that age, as she very much wanted the puppy forever and not just for Christmas Day.

She had tried to hide her disappointment from her parents, not wanting to seem ungrateful to them or to Santa, but her lack of usual hyperactive enthusiasm made her mother suspicious. The pang of terror- as her mum caught her crying- was so strong that it echoed to the present, tightening her chest. It wasn't fear of making her mum angry, or fear of being deemed ungrateful, but fear of hurting and disappointing her parents.

Knowing exactly what her daughter was upset over, Haidee's mum cradled her, stroking her hair and speaking softly to her.

"You'll get a dog when you're older." Haidee remembered her saying, "Sometimes, the things we want we have to get ourselves, but what's important is that we are given the things we need. A roof over our head, food on our plate and a family that loves us."

It didn't make sense to Haidee at the time, as she already had all those things, so she didn't need them at all. Now, while she was quite content not to have a dog that relied on her and while her pitiful adult life made her grateful for having food, shelter, friends and family, she still had something, *someone*, she really desperately wanted: her mum.

Preoccupied by her thoughts, her auto-pilot self had walked her into the middle of Inverleith park. It was the route she usually took to Leah's flat, but never alone in the dark. There were a few other people about, dog walkers, a cyclist, a group of friends, but it still didn't feel the safest. There was an endless stretch of black, barely lit by the dull street lamps. Trees were scattered at the side of the pavement, leering at her as she passed.

Keeping her wits about her, she listened for footsteps nearby. The trees were large enough for someone to hide behind, and she heard too many stories of women being attacked in these settings to think it unlikely. Leah's keys were already in her hand, poking through her fingers like claws, ready to swipe down any threat. She sped up, all the while feeling that constant sensation of being watched.

Each footstep went further and further, faster and faster, until she was practically running down the path. She looked over her shoulder and all around, it was just her in the park now, from what she could see, but her paranoia was getting the better of her. Instincts couldn't be ignored, no matter if they had been alerting her to a delusion for the last few weeks. Even a broken clock is right twice a day.

The sounds of loud scratches on the concrete forced her to leap forward, spinning on her heel, brandishing her key-shaped claws in the air. It had sounded like someone had attempted to throw something jagged at her, but it had rolled across the ground. Her eyes darted all across the ground, until she finally saw it, still moving.

It was just a rat.

Relief soothed her shaking body. Rats might have caused a saner person to freak out, but Haidee was too preoccupied with so many fears and worries that she had to prioritise. Rodents she could handle, rapists she could not. She hurried on to the safety of Leah's flat, expecting her to be there when she got home, but what she found was a place in distress.

The door was unlocked, as it usually was when Leah was home, but when Haidee called her name there was no reply. At first, the living room and kitchen seemed to be in their usual messy state, but upon closer inspection, the mess looked more like debris. The remnants of a few plates lay scattered on the carpet, the wallpaper had been scratched by the impact. One of the kitchen cupboard handles had come loose, its arched bar dangled over a bloodied kitchen towel. A stool by the breakfast bar had been knocked over, and the petite Christmas tree leaned precariously against the window.

Haidee ran back out into the stairwell, pulling out her phone to call 999, until she saw a text. It was Leah: "At hospital, minor emergency, don't worry. Flats a tip, soz. Cya tonite xxx"

She tried to call Leah, as the very little information brought her no comfort, but it went straight to voicemail every time.

Slowly, and with great caution, she re-entered the flat. Her imagination tried to make sense of the scene being a "Minor emergency."

Scenario one: Leah had been drying two dishes at once, accidentally threw them at the wall, then in a rage, pushed the stool and Christmas tree over. She then punched the handle, causing it to break, and hurt her hand in the process, using the dish towel to soak up the blood. This was unlikely.

Scenario two: Leah was absolutely hammered, after drinks with her workmates, fell off the stool and stumbled into the Christmas tree. She then broke the handle on the cupboard and then threw the dishes at the wall in frustration. When trying to clean up her mess, she hurt her hand and used the dish towel to stop the bleeding. A little more plausible.

Scenario three: Leah was doing dishes when she saw a *spider* on the wall. It had crawled in the window, by the Christmas tree, so she threw something at it, toppling over the tree. This only scared the spider, it began to scurry along the floor, Haidee tried to stand on the stool but this put too much weight on it, causing the stool to fall one way and her to fall against the kitchen cupboard, yanking the top of the handle from its screw. As she saw the spider clamber up the wall, she grabbed the nearest thing to throw at it- a plate. There was no brown-legged gunge stuck to the wall or floor, so it was safe to assume Leah missed, meaning the spider had scurried into another hiding place. Leah realised she hit her head when she had fallen against the cupboard, so mopped up the blood with the dish towel and then went to hospital to make sure she wasn't concussed. This one hundred percent made sense for Leah.

The likeliness of scenario three did ease Haidee's concerns to a point, but while her fears and worries made no time for rats, they did make room for spiders. She tiptoed around the flat carefully, making sure to scan the bedroom as she first entered it and to shake out her pyjamas before she put them on.

Still, she was anxious. She tried to push through each day, with the hopes that her faith in reality would return, a hope that was crumbling beneath her frantic thoughts. The nagging feeling never really left, and her mind was determined to summon the image of The Watcher, pulling at the thread of her sanity, unravelling her mental health. She needed Leah.

Determination ignited inside her, awakening the confident and independent Haidee that had laid dormant for the last few weeks. She was done telling herself over and over again what was real and what was not, what was paranoia or stress or anxiety or all three. In that moment, she made a deal with herself: to call out The Watcher one more time. Once he didn't appear, she'd be done with it. No more fear, no more dread, no more doubts.

'I know... You're here.' she spoke so softly, she could barely hear herself. It was embarrassing, like a little girl scared to say "Bloody Mary" three times in the mirror. She forced a shout from her chest, 'I know you're here, so show yourself!'

She whipped her head around, to where she felt the nagging feeling pull her, the corner of the room where the lamp's light didn't reach. There was nobody there. She dropped to her knees to look under the bed, nobody there either.

A triumphant, and slightly maniacal, laugh bellowed out from her lungs. She was free. A deal was a deal and the anxiety she had felt was leaving her body, one giggle at a time.

Until the giggling stopped.

Fear held its invisible hand over her mouth. She couldn't laugh, speak or even breathe. The terror was sudden but not random. She had felt it, the warm breath, push against the hairs on her neck, raising every single one.

Every muscle was stiff, as though she had been scared to death and the rigor mortis had already set in. The thread had been pulled too far, her mental state was completely undone, she was paralysed. Her eyes were the only thing that could move, and they did, to look at the small mirror on Leah's desk. It was angled towards the ceiling, but it caught the reflection of Haidee's forehead, and two unforgettable eyes staring right at her.

Adrenaline broke the paralysis, and Haidee found herself racing through to the living room, slamming the door shut behind her, holding the handle, ready to use all her strength to keep her nightmare locked away.

A pale light breezed out the bottom of the door, as another light appeared in the middle of the room, pulling her attention away.

There he was.

As the bright light dimmed, the only thing left lighting the room was the softly glowing cracks of lightning that appeared from his back.

'Of course I'm here,' He smiled, 'I never really left.'

Haidee fell to the ground, too shaken to scream or cry. All she did was watch as his electric wings crackled out of existence, plunging them both into darkness. His silhouette moved towards her, but again she was paralysed. There was no hope in outrunning a creature that could appear anywhere within a flash of light.
She awaited the horrors he was bound to inflict on her, certain he would slip her into another coma or worse, a sleep she would never awake from.

Instead, he flicked the light switch, making himself visible once more. She stared up at him, wide-eyed like a rabbit chased down by a fox. He gazed back down, and began to back up towards Leah's favourite armchair, where he sat in anticipation.

Minutes went by with the two just staring at each other. Her breathing steadied with every second, as her mind knitted itself back into a functional state. He leaned back, crossing his leg in an odd way, so that his right foot balanced on his left knee and he could fiddle with his shoe laces. All his actions were slow, which he made sure of, showing Haidee that he wasn't about to make any sudden moves. Understandingly untrusting, she was certain this was a trap.

'Why are you doing this to me?' she tried to speak bravely, but it came out as a whimper.

He stopped fiddling with his laces, 'I'm not doing anything, Haidee.'

'You're... Haunting me.' She squeezed her eyes shut, as if that would force him out of existence, 'I don't deserve this.'

'It's not about what you deserve, Haidee.' As she opened her eyes again she saw sympathy in his, 'It's about what's meant to be. You were given seventeen more years, which you should be grateful for. Some souls would give the world and more just for one day more with the people they love. But it's your time to go, Haidee.'

It was hard to digest what he was saying, but Haidee felt that she had no other choice but to listen.

'And this is as good a time as any, considering how hard it's gotten for you. I've seen you struggle to do your job when you had one, no struggle to find one. You've set up camp in your friend's flat, you have no means to rely on yourself, and I know that's not the life you want, Haidee.'

'Stop saying my name.' she snapped, half out of anger, half out of distress.'If you really are Death come to collect, why haven't you just done it with the click of your fingers? Why did I get seventeen more years? Why are you fucking with my head?'

'Someone intervened.' he said more sternly. The look on her face asked the question for her which he quickly answered, 'Someone who had no business intervening. Now, I have to right his wrong, anyway I can, but I don't want to hurt you.'

'Don't act like a nice guy and then threaten me.'

'It's a warning, no a threat. All I want to do is pass you on peacefully. What if you could have anything, do anything, be anywhere right now?'

She thought about it, involuntarily: her wants, her wishes, her desires. The more she did so, the more a decision began to form and, as it formed, it projected onto the world around her. The snow flakes hailed down and settled on the carpet. Tall fir trees became visible through the walls. The bright blues and pinks and greens sliced through the ceiling: the Borealis Race was dancing above her head. A front-row view of the Northern Lights.

'Haidee, name anything and it's yours.' he spoke animatedly as Leah's flat began to fade from her sight.

She could feel it this time. She could feel the cold Icelandic air push down into her lungs. She could see her breath as a fog in front of her. She could feel the wet kisses of snowflakes on her face, fingers and toes. It felt real this time. Yet, her heart was numb to it.

'I want you to stop saying my name.' she demanded, 'And I want you to switch this thing off, whatever this is.'

His lively expression fell into one of disdain as the snow and the trees and the Northern Lights began to evaporate. They had returned to the warmth of Leah's flat.

She wasn't sure what to make of her Watcher anymore. There was a kindness that radiated from him, something her heart was willing to trust, but as he said before "I am Death." She didn't understand many things about this situation but she understood that his goal was to take her life and that was all she needed to know. He would tempt her with illusions and mess with her head until he got his way.

'I'm never going to let you take me.' she said, 'I'll always choose life, however bad it gets, you can't bribe me with imaginary things.' She gestured to the kitchen, which had a wooden rack with five types of kitchen knives, 'If you want me dead you'll have to do something old-fashioned, like stab me.'

The tension had become so deafening that now all they heard was silence. She waited for him to leave, thinking she may have won, thinking this nightmare had finally been banished. He got up and moved to the kitchen. Panic punched her deep in the stomach and she pounced to her feet. The slicing sound of metal against wood tore through her nerves as he removed the thickest knife from the rack.

'Why didn't I think of this myself?' He approached her, eyes wild, face straight.

She tried to run around to the other side of the couch- he quickly side-stepped, grabbing her. She shrieked before he threw her against the wall. He came at her- her fists fired at him, managing to strike him a few times but he was resilient. He grabbed one wrist then the other, with just one hand, and pinned them above her head. Kicking and screaming with all the ferocity she could muster, she pushed away her pacifist nature and called for any violent action she could take. If she could reach, she would have bit his nose off.

Stepping on her, his heavy shoe weighed down on her bare feet. She let out a cry of pain as the edges of his heels dug into her toes. Then, he held the tip of the knife less than an inch from her throat.

She wanted to keep fighting. She wanted to thrash her body out of his hold. She wanted to live. However, she knew if she kept trying to fight she'd end up slicing her own throat.

'You really shouldn't have suggested this.' he said as she cried hysterically, the hairs of her throat brushing against the blade, 'But I'm no so cruel. If you let me pass you on it will be peaceful. No pain or knives involved. I can take you to a dream world. You can have your bucket list done in seconds.'

Each word summoned a shudder. She was going to die. It was happening- her death was about to happen. This was it, she never had a choice. Death would take her by force. She didn't want to die. She couldn't die- she wasn't ready- it wasn't right. Trepidation had struck her heart and she was unable to speak. Her cry was rendered silent.

'Which is it, Haidee?' his whisper grazed against her ear, 'I can pass you on or I can really kill you. It's your choice.'

It wasn't much of one. Die peacefully or die painfully still had the end result. In that moment, she hated him. She had never truly hated anyone before and now, in her last moment, she had become capable of it. He was cruel and vicious and worthy of all hatred.

Maybe the best decision for her would be to go peacefully, to just accept her fate and meet it gracefully. However, her pride intervened, screaming inside her: *fuck this bastard.*

'You'll have to get your hands bloody.' she spat, 'I will never *agree* to die!'

The grip on her wrists tightened. His heels pressed harder on her toes.

'Are you sure?' His stare was intense, invoking more fear from her, and yet, an equal amount of courage.

'Yes.' she said, as stubborn, determined and proud as she had been her entire life.

The cold metal blade of the knife met her skin, inviting goosebumps to the surface. She exhaled carefully, blowing air against the face of her Watcher, her hunter, her end.

He let her fall to the ground, then casually waltzed over to the kitchen area where he placed the clean knife back in its holder. Haidee blinked away her tears, trying to steady her trembling body as she checked her neck to make sure he hadn't sliced it so quickly that she hadn't noticed.

The skin on her neck was wet from tears, but very much intact. He walked back over to her, she just watched in awe as he picked her up by the waist and sat her on the couch. He took his place opposite her.

'You didn't kill me.' the words wandered from her mouth, while her mind was still trying to make its way back to her.

Guilt seized The Watcher. It was clear what trauma he had just inflicted. He thought about reaching out for her hand, an attempt to soothe her in an even bigger attempt to soothe his conscience. Yet, he was aware his inconsistent attitude had only made the situation harder for both of them and could continue to do so.

'If you were trapped in a burning house for hours on end, you'd come out burnt to the bone, but you would still come out. If you got hit by a train, you'd break every bone in your body, fracture your skull and have your muscles torn apart, but you'd still survive. If I had slit your throat, you'd bleed out until you were within an inch of your life, but you'd still have that inch.' Realising she was still staring into space, she turned to face him and tried her best to absorb what he was saying, 'Death isn't a bad thing. It comes for you to spare you from any of that pain. It comes for you when it's your time.' He held out his hand, 'It's time.'

She stared down at his hand that hovered over the coffee table. There were two mugs on the table. One was Haidee's, a cream egg mug that she had gotten with an Easter egg one year. The other was Leah's with a picture of a pig on it, and the phrase "You're a Babe." They were both filled with tea, Leah must have filled them before her adventure with the spider. She never even had to ask Leah to make her a cup of tea.

Without another thought, she grabbed one of the mugs and hurled it at The Watcher's head. The remainder of tea cartwheeled out before he caught the mug in the palm of his hand.

'Arse!' she barked.

He placed the mug back on the table and wiped the splatter of tea from his face, 'That's Leah's favourite.'

She didn't care. In an instant, she was at the door, holding it open. He glared at her astonished. She wouldn't look at him.

'You can't make me go.' he said.

She didn't acknowledge him. Continuing to stand rigidly, she held the door open and allowed a slight breeze to enter from the stairwell.

After a few moments, he walked over to her and positioned himself in her line of sight, preventing her from ignoring him. He was about to make another attempt to persuade her but her words pushed his own back into his mouth.

'If you couldn't kill me, why put me through all that?' her speech was fragile, each syllable she uttered wobbled, yet, they slammed against him with a rage that she couldn't suppress.

'I thought it was worth a try.' His smile was bittersweet and almost innocent, unlike the actions in question.

Her lips echoed his, 'Worth a try?' He witnessed the endurance break within her before seeing her palm smack across his face.

There was a look of surprise on her face. After just witnessing his reflexes with the mug, it was impossible to believe he had let her slap him. Before his constant contradictory actions could confuse her any further, she grabbed him and shoved him out the door.

He watched in bewilderment as nonsensical sentences spilled from her mouth, with the core message of how he was sick and twisted. The tears leapt from her eyes as the profanities leapt from her mouth. The door slammed shut straight after.

A neighbour peered out their door for a moment but she would not see the messenger of Death standing in the hallway. He placed his hands against the door that had just been slammed on him, feeling it downwards until he was crouched on the floor.

Haidee was on the other side with her back against it and her crying head tucked between her knees. He pressed his ear against the wood, torturing himself with the sound of her sobs. It filled him with an addictive guilt. It was addictive to his conscience that knew he deserved to feel responsible for the pain he had caused. If Faith's signature wasn't enough of an obstacle already, he knew the guilt would prove to be.

Truthfully, he had not intended to scare her. He had intended to slit her throat, knowing that she'd be begging for death just to escape the pain that no mortal being was ever supposed to endure. It would have been job done. Another name off the list. Although it was the logical thing to do, when it came down to it, he could not handle exposing her to pain worse than death.

He had only had to cross over a few living souls before and they weren't like Haidee at all. It was a matter of mercy for them, a mercy that they had prayed for; people in their sick bed, doomed and without hope. Listening to the pain that he had caused this life, that was so determined to live, compelled him to pray for the strength he needed to force this woman to accept death.

A loud bang answered him, forcing him to jolt away from the door, followed by Haidee shouting, 'Fuck off!'

She could sense him on the other side of the door like she could sense his stare. With a flash that emitted so brightly it spilled under the door, he left.

The distance travelled wasn't far, he was now on a rooftop where he could see into Leah's flat and watch Haidee's turmoil from afar. The perfect view for brewing in his guilt. Tragically, he did not know, that even from that distance, she could feel his eyes on her. He did not know that he was still inflicting torture, not only onto himself but onto her. That was, until she yanked the curtains shut.

CHAPTER 13

A Little City of Edinburgh

The surroundings injected Haidee's mind with a sense of déjà vu. Despite the absence of chandeliers, antique decor and trellising against walls, she was certain that she was sat in *The Maple*. The location and layout were exactly the same with only minor changes to the interior.

The Copper Blossom had a lighter tone, boasting cream brick walls and floral patterns on the chairs. She sat with her father and Moira in a cosy wee booth with flowers as a centrepiece. The menu was just as fancy but much less vague than *The Maple's*; you knew exactly what you were getting.

She was convinced the place had been the inspiration in The Watcher's design. It was completely to her taste and undoubtedly most people's. Still, she wondered how her Watcher knew the blueprints to her ideal life. She felt like more than just an open book; it was as though her pages had been ripped out, highlighted and annotated.

She tried her best to ignore her feelings of vulnerability for the sake of enjoying her three-course meal, paid for by the bank of dad. It was a struggle, considering what had happened just a few nights ago. A little noise, a sudden move or even a gentle breeze sent her into panic mode. Leah could sense that something had happened, but Haidee knew that, even with her closest friend, the truth wouldn't be believed. In the end, she told her it was nervous jitters and her anxiety. Although Leah was unconvinced, she would be a hypocrite to call her out. It wasn't a war on a spider that led Leah to the hospital, but when Haidee asked for the real story, she was shrugged off and told it was just absolute clumsiness. Yet, Leah had returned without a scratch on her, making the bloodied dish towel an even bigger mystery. Haidee could hazard a guess: Pete was involved.

If Leah wouldn't talk about it, Haidee wouldn't pry. She had done so in the past, and it had been at the risk of their friendship. She was just grateful Leah wasn't hurt.
She was also grateful for the gifts her dad and Moira had given her. The main one being a coat, which she desperately needed as her thin faux-leather jacket barely protected her from the cold. Moira made sure to spare no expense, it was cream and cashmere with faux-fur lining. When Haidee tried it on, she felt as though she was being snuggled by a bear. Other gifts included: holeless blouses, holeless jeans and a long grey cardigan that did have two holes, one on each shoulder. However, these were *fashionable* holes.

Despite all the wonderful gifts that Moira had clearly picked out, she could not disguise how uncomfortable she was. Her smile was large and welcoming but her eyes were screaming in distress. Haidee could relate. Neither of them really wanted to be sat opposite each other. It wasn't that the two disliked each other, but it was awkward being, legally, family that had barely spoken two words to each other.

'So, the offer still stands...' her dad started, again, on his quest to convince her. 'We have the guest bedroom all set up for you, so don't hesitate to come home.'

'I'm fine where I am.' Haidee said with a mouthful of mashed tatties, 'I really appreciate the prezzies though.'

'I had fun shopping for you.' Moira finally found words to speak, 'We should go shopping together, my treat.' There was immediate regret in her eyes. She would have to find more things to talk about if they were alone together.

'I think you've bought enough for me.' Haidee promptly relieved her of step-mum duties, 'I won't have to go shopping in a long time. Apart from food.'

'Oh, well I can't help you there, I order our groceries online.' She shrugged, clearly fumbling for actual conversation, 'But if you're ever short on food, I'll order a delivery for you?'
'It's fine Moira.' Haidee was beginning to find their exchange comedic, 'Thank you for the thought, though.'

She felt relaxed by Haidee's last comment, enough to continue eating her lasagna, which she had just been prodding at for the last few minutes.

Her dad seemed less than impressed, 'No. If you're struggling for food, you come home. You should be home. I'm not convinced that Leah's looking after you properly.'

'That's 'cause she's not looking after me. That's because she realises that I'm an independent twenty-four-year-old woman who can take care of myself,' she said, 'I might have had a couple of hiccups but I'm fine, now.'

Her dad grumbled to himself. She understood his grouchy manner was a result of his concern for her but she hadn't much patience for it. Both the nagging feeling and the sensation of the knife against her throat remained with her. She had bigger concerns than his bad mood.

Concerns; which lingered after her, long after dinner and long after she was back in Leah's flat.

She was alone again, Leah was at her work's Christmas party and wouldn't return for hours. The Watcher's gaze felt much weaker. Perhaps he'd finally disappeared or maybe she had just gotten used to the feeling but, either way, it meant she didn't know where he was. Death had become a spider, hiding somewhere in the room, ready to jump on her as she opened the cupboard doors or scurry up her leg as she slipped on her shoes.

Everything she saw in the flat prompted the memory of that dire moment. Her throat would close at the thought of the blade's sharpness. The bruises on her toes would ache as she felt his weight and his heels push down on them, her wrists still felt bound by his grip. If it was only to instill fear into her, it worked. She knew it was only a matter of time before he tried another wicked game.

The dread could not be tolerated, she needed out of that room.

Daundering around Edinburgh, she passed couples and friends, linked by arms, hips and intertwined fingers. Her new coat warded away the icy air from her body but her face could not swerve winter's frosty touch. She felt she was the only one who noticed how cold it was, everyone else drew warmth from each other's laughter and smiles.

Edinburgh felt untouchable. All these beautiful moments, people who were going somewhere or coming back from somewhere else, experiencing everything the city had to offer; Haidee could never be one of those people. She didn't have the money. She didn't have the health. She could look but never touch. Her gaze was that of a ghost's, envying the living.

She lovingly patted the walls of old buildings, bricks upon bricks that had stood strong for centuries. How many centuries had her Watcher witnessed? It seemed possible that he saw them being built. It may have been that he watched people live in these houses, watched them grow old and grey and then took them from this world.

A feeling, very little but incredibly loud in that moment, thought it might not be such a terrible thing to let him take her, to bring her peace. Immediately, she convinced herself she never felt that way, that the thought had never crossed her mind and she went on haunting the streets of the capital.

She took steps leading into a narrow area, dimly lit by distant lamp posts. Her back turned on the castle. She knew these steps would lead her to the Grassmarket; a cobbled plaza which sounded as though it were filled with many merry drunks.

That nagging feeling emerged once again. She could feel eyes on her. She looked over her shoulder to see five sets of green eyes staring her down; it was stenciled graffiti on the wall. She kept moving, trying to out-walk the horrid memory that was catching up to her. Her throat began to close as her heart banged on her chest, like someone trapped. She hurried to the Grassmarket but, as she turned the corner, she saw a wall.

Not a single brick had existed there before.

The united light from the pubs and restaurants, lamp posts and fairy lights, reached over the wall. It made the contents of the alley way visible, only faintly. She could see litter; an Irn Bru can scrunched up in the corner with leaves and dirt; a train ticket from Shotts to Edinburgh and the odd unidentifiable sweet wrapper. Weeds grew through cracks in the path and moss up the walls. Behind her, another wall had suddenly appeared, leaving only one way out. To her left was an archway which had been bricked up long ago, but tonight, all that filled it was a darkness.

If you had asked Haidee's dad: she had a terrible fear of the dark when she was wee. Haidee would argue against that. She had never been afraid of the dark, she was afraid of what could be hiding in the dark. Her mind would go wild with thoughts of monsters and demons, waiting and watching her like prey. Now she knew what kind of monster was watching. She could feel its gaze raise every hair on her body.

However, it was a different feeling, heavier and tighter. The Watcher's stare that she had become familiar with felt more pinching while this one was like a hand grabbing the back of her neck. Her gut told her that the eyes on her had never seen her before. Her gut told her: this was not her Watcher.

There was another, a creature that could be just as brutal, if not more so. She refused to be afraid. He couldn't kill her, so she doubted this ghoul could. She walked under the arch, immediately feeling the icy air pierce through her cashmere armour.

Every instinct begged her to run, and she almost gave into the plea, but on looking back she saw there was no longer a place to run to. She was in over her head. This was another psychotic mind game and she was not in any kind of mood to play along.

'I know you're watching.' she hissed into the darkness, the void swallowed the mist from her breath, 'I don't know who you are, and I don't care. Get. This. Over. With.'

Reaching both hands out, she felt for the walls and carefully shuffled forward. Something *felt* back. Many things felt back, with their many legs. On her hands, legs, face, hair, she could feel them scrambling across her skin. She shrieked as they crawled all over her, underneath her clothes, into her ears, up her nose- she forced herself to shut her mouth before they had a chance to clamber in there as well.

Spiders.

An agonising hum was the only sound she could make as she slapped them away, feeling their gooey insides on her goosebumps as she squished them. The spiders clung to the strands of her hair. The spiders tickled their way down her boots. The spiders raced down her spine. There was no part of her that had been spared by the spiders' touch.

She ran further into the dark, flailing her arms in front of her, in an attempt to find the creature responsible for her terror. A dim light outlined what lay before her. A very narrow and steep alleyway was made just visible. Her knees wobbled together as her heels took the weight of each step, careful not to slip. Her pace was cut to a quarter of what it once was. She hated steep paths and roads, even though they were everywhere, as every place in Scotland had to be built on a hill or a mound. It would be so easy to slip. Each time one foot left the ground, panic strummed her heart, giving her chaos a rhythm.

As every muscle tensed in her venture downhill, she began to hear crumbling. The walls at either side of the alleyway tilted towards one another, collapsing as they met. Haidee tried to outrun the falling debris- but the steepness tripped her up and she fell onto her back, watching the rubble dive towards her. She cried out, shielding her head with her arms and her stomach with her shins.

Instead of the beating of bricks on her bones, she was surprised to feel the trickle of rain. She opened her eyes to find herself beside the arch she had entered, which was again bricked up, and the wall to the Grassmarket had vanished. No spiders, no steep hills, no collapsing buildings. All she felt now was complete and utter relief. She pushed herself up from the damp floor and wandered into the Grassmarket excited to see other people after what she had experienced.

There was not a single soul. The pubs were still lit and the doors were wide open but, as she investigated, she saw no one inside. As she walked up the road by Princes Street Gardens and St. Cuthbert's Cemetery, she did not pass anyone on foot or in a vehicle. She wandered onto Lothian Road where there were no buses, no taxis, no busy Christmas shoppers waiting at the crossings, not even the man who usually sold the big issue on the corner.

She turned onto Princes Street, the busiest place in Edinburgh, but it had met the same fate. Not a single person stood there but Haidee. She walked passed the gate to the graveyard, careful not to glance into it. This whole situation felt reminiscent of her previous escape from Death's illusion. Her mind was once again trapped in a cage.

However, she noted the main differences: her Watcher's fantasy world was just that, a fantasy. Good, lovely, joyous things coated in sugar and wrapped up in string. This was horrific: walking down Princes Street towards a deserted Christmas Market, knowing that the spinning Ferris Wheel was abandoned and that there would be nobody there in the aisles of the market.

It was one of her fears. A recurring nightmare. A common one for people to have: being the last person on Earth. It was the same with the dark and the spiders and the steep narrow alleyway that collapsed on top of her: they were all long-time fears of hers. Which meant she wasn't alone. Which meant there was, at least, one other being in her mind with her.

She entered the Christmas Market, passed unmanned stalls, following the feeling of the stare, anxiously peering around each corner.

'Dee!' The voice came from above. She looked up and saw Leah looking down at her from a glassless window of the Walter Scott Monument, her face covered in blood.

A terrible, awful fear it was- she immediately ran into the tower, scared for her friend. Then, she slowed down as she moved up the spiral staircase, realising that the

Leah she saw was another fake. She silently scolded herself, dreading what she had just gotten herself into. There was no decision from this point on, she looked behind her to see another brick wall. The only way was up.

Upon reaching the top, the fake Leah had disappeared. Haidee moved towards the window where she had seen her standing and peered out at the city that had now been swallowed by pitch-blackness. Only the light of the moon and the stars granted her sight.

A few muffled taps sounded behind her, the sound of heels against 19th-century stone. Gripping onto the ledge of the window, she cautiously looked over her shoulder and there he was, her Watcher. In his hand was the same knife he had held to her throat. He sliced the air, the lashing sounds forcing her stomach to jerk inwards. She clutched at her chest in an attempt to ease her racing heart, but the shrinking distance between them prevented her from doing so. The room was pushing them towards each other.

'Leave me alone.' she demanded, managing to keep herself calm despite her heart thrashing against her chest. There was no hope that her demand would be met but she couldn't think of what else to do.

He lunged towards her- she tried to dodge but he had her. Half her body was suspended, her spine bent over the ledge, she was clinging to his clothes for dear life. Once again, he had that knife against her throat but, as she stared into the eyes of her horror, she noticed a difference in him. His eyes were wilder and his face was much more gaunt. His paleness hung by two cheekbones. There was a hunger in his eyes, a hunger to watch her suffer. Within his fist, the handle of the knife, ready in the air to come down upon her.

This time, he truly looked like Death. This was not her Watcher at all.

It was a reluctant realisation she had, for she could, so easily, have let herself believe him to be a bloodthirsty reaper. Yet, she was familiar with the gaze of her Watcher. Whenever they crossed paths, he would look like a deer in headlights. On his face was a sympathetic brow whenever he spoke. She saw the agonising determination he possessed when he had held that knife to her throat before. He was determined to endure the sight of her pain. He never hungered after her misery.

Her hatred for him was justified, but it was unable to turn him into a monster. His actions were unforgivable but she could not deny what she had witnessed within him; a conscience. This wasn't her Watcher; this was just fear. This was a nightmare that had taken form in flesh. With that knowledge, the imminent threat, that she had felt she was in, vanished. Her fear vanished. The nightmare version of her Watcher vanished.

She turned herself to face over the edge of the window, the city remained dark and empty. Her nightmare wasn't over. She couldn't comprehend what fear of hers was left to use against her, until the ground began to rumble.

The instant dread she felt led her to where the steps should have been. It was just a stone floor now. There was no way out. She thought about curling up in a ball in the corner, it might be her best chance of survival.

A loud crunch of the 200-year-old stone sounded beneath her and the monument began to tilt towards the clocktower of the Balmoral Hotel, causing her to slide to the opposite window. She grappled at the edges of its stone frame. The urge to curl up grew stronger but logic told her that it wouldn't help. She knew deep down that the nightmare wouldn't end until she had faced her fears.

The Walter Scott Monument was falling. Haidee held her breath as her body became light during the descent. She refused to close her eyes as she heard the crash and crumble of the clocktower, as it was struck by the monument's spire. Rubble rained upon Waverley Mall. The roar of destruction became deafening. Her eyes welled up and her body trembled uncontrollably as she prepared herself to meet with that rubble.

Then she heard the rush of a car- A muffled sigh of a bus door as it opened. There was talking, a lot of talking. She looked up hoping to see the Grassmarket where she had left reality but, instead, she found herself in the exact spot where she was meant to collide with the ground. The city was no longer empty or dark. As she turned on her back, she saw the Walter Scott Monument standing tall, looming over the citizens of Edinburgh that had returned. To her relief there were hundreds and hundreds of people all around.

But then came her absolute worst nightmare.

Those hundreds and hundreds of people were all looking at *her*.

CHAPTER 14
Hark The Herald Angels Sing

Haidee McLean's biggest fear: going crazy and everybody knowing it.

She pushed herself up from the pavement, still feeling the tiny pitter-patters of spiders all over her body. There were no bruises or broken bones, no evidence of her fall. The surrounding crowd was staring at her, some whispering to each other. A mother pulled her pram back as her child cried, another person ran away and mentioned they were going to get help. One man shouted, light-heartedly, about her maybe having one too many hot toddies. Some people laughed but others looked at her like she was a bomb about to go off in the middle of their happy festivities.

An old lady approached her guardedly and took her trembling hand. Her eyes were kind and filled with concern, her voice was clear but soft enough so that she would not be startled, 'Did ye take somin' ye shouldnae 'ave, pet?'

Haidee was still waiting for her senses to fully return and it took some time to register what the woman was saying. Some of the crowd began to move on. Others stared at her expectantly, unsure whether they should stay, in case they could assist in some way, or leave to give her space. She was a fly caught in a web; unable to move, awaiting demise.

'Should we get ye tae ay hospital?' the woman asked.

It was the last thing she needed. Her dad would carry her out of the hospital and to his and Moira's home; locking her in the guest bedroom, condemning her to watch every soap omnibus repeatedly. She would try to say that she was fine and run off and pretend nothing happened, but the shock had rendered her mute. She could see a police officer approaching her out of the corner of her eye. This was it, they would haul her away to the looney bin.

A hand gently rested on her shoulder, 'She's been a bit under the weather, lately.' a faintly-familiar voice answered on her behalf, 'The doctor gave her something a wee bit strong and she wandered off.' He patted her head as though she was a little lost puppy, 'Sorry if my sister worried any of you.'

The crowd began to disperse and the old woman looked very relieved, 'Well I hope you feel better, pet.' She squeezed Haidee's hand and moved away with the rest of the crowd.

Haidee looked up towards her alleged brother to see spiralling dark locks of hair, 'I'll take you back home.' He smiled offering his arm. Haidee took it.

She knew that she knew him. There was a familiarity around his black mesh of hair and his all-knowing smirk. It took nine minutes of walking, holding onto his arm to keep her balance, before she finally placed him in her memory.

'You're that creepy guy from that, uh, coffee place.' she finally spoke, but her words were shaking just as much as her body was.

He grinned proudly over his recognisability. 'I shouldn't have talked to you that day. I'm in a lot of trouble because of you. I think a lot of people are.'

There was a question in her stare. His casual demeanor said that he had no intention of answering, just yet. He didn't speak again until they were in a more concealed location; following twisting, turning roads in a residential area.

'I'm impressed you managed to face *Fear*. I've never known anyone to do that and keep their sanity. Though, maybe I'm speaking too soon.'

The minute she realised what he was referring to, she pulled away from him, stumbling towards a lamp post to keep her upright. It wasn't enough. She fell to the floor, watching the world around her fizz like static on a television. 'You know...' Her eyes welled up with tears, 'You know what happened to me?'

He approached her, removing a bottle of Irn Bru from his large leather satchel, 'Drink it.'

She shook her head.

'It's sealed. I bought it just for you, I thought you might feel a bit faint afterwards. You need the sugar.'

She glowered up at him. It was good practice to keep her guard up with strangers, a rule she had stuck by since childhood, but there was no use in that now. If he wanted to do anything to her, she was helpless. Her body yearned for the sugary liquid, knowing it would have a medicinal effect on her dizziness. Whoever this man was, she had no choice but to trust him.

'Have a little *faith* in your fellow human being.' he urged her, 'It's an important faith to have.'

Within seconds, she had downed the drink, then closed her mouth to muffle the sound of a burp. She moaned uncomfortably, waiting for the wooziness to subside.

'You know who I am?' he asked.

She shook her head again, 'But I can guess *what* you are.'

'And that is?'

'Another messenger of Death.'

The man did not attempt to hold back his laughter, 'I would normally be insulted, but I'll plead ignorance on your behalf, on this occasion.'

'You're like him though. Whoever he is- my not-so-human stalker.' His expression encouraged her to believe she was right, 'You were the one who told me to call out the person watching me... You already knew.'

'I love the sound of the penny dropping.' Excitement prompted him to clap and stomp his feet.

'You did this! You got inside my head!' She began to tear up again, 'You scared me shitless!'

'Nope.' He raised a finger in protest, 'That wasn't me. That's not my domain nor is it your stalker's. He had someone else do that...' Gradually, his all-knowing smirk returned, as if someone had just whispered a secret in his ear. Without moving his head, he looked down the street, and Haidee knew exactly why he chose to look there. Her mind had been so rattled by her terrors that she barely noticed the nagging sensation calling for her to face the same direction.

'He's here.' she bubbled to herself, witnessing The Watcher materialise through the darkness.

The man gestured to her but addressed The Watcher, 'Do you have no *shame*? Or maybe we should arrange a meeting with her?'

Her Watcher stood silently, doing what he did best: watching Haidee. This time, he watched with pity in his eyes.

'He can't hurt me?' she asked the man for reassurance.

'Oh, he definitely can.' the man said, 'But he won't.' Offering his hand, he helped her off the floor and squeezed her shoulder in support, 'I suggest you go home.'

'I have questions.' She tugged at his coat.

'And I have answers, for another day.' He gently nudged her off.

If she hadn't been so drained from her ordeal, and if her Watcher's stare wasn't so unnerving to her, then she would have stayed and demanded the answers at once. However, her body cried out for some rest and her mind begged for peace.

Reluctantly, she began to walk towards the road, having to get a little bit closer to The Watcher before she could put as much distance between them as possible. As she walked past him, they made eye contact and he felt it necessary to say, 'I am sorry. For everything I have done... and for everything I'll *have* to do.'

Haidee pulled away from his gaze and hurried off, swaying from dizziness as she did so. The worst thing about his apology: a part of her believed he was truly sorry. As she neared the corner, she stole a quick glance back, only for the two men to be nowhere in sight.

Calmness settled upon her as she felt that, for the first time in a long time, nobody was watching.

She was free, if only for a night.

CHAPTER 15
Angels From The Realm Of Glory

Anxiety-induced cleaning sessions: nothing motivates a person more than complete and utter panic.

Haidee scrubbed down the counters vigorously, as if to scrub away the memories of last night. The hoover devoured every little bit of fluff, every tiny wee crumb on the carpet, but not a single tremor was lifted from her body. Nooks and crannies could no longer shelter fuzzles of dust, but the fissures in her sanity housed horrific thoughts- the main one being; what is going to happen next?

'Dee!' Leah yelled over the music that Haidee had blasted to drown out her thoughts.

She turned the volume down, 'What's up?'

'Ye... Didnae move any ay ma stuff while cleaning, did ye?' Concern had pinched Leah's brows together.

'No, have you lost something?'

She ran her hand through her hair, ruffling it as if an idea of where it could be would fall from the blondeness.

'Leah?'

'It's, uh, just... Ye didnae borrow money?' Her voice was hushed now, strained even, as if each word was trying to stretch over an obstacle.

'No, not without asking, I don't do that.'

'I ken, I ken... But there's... Nobody else, Dee...'

'How much are you missing?'

Leah didn't reply at first, clearly reading Haidee's behaviour and trying to make a decision of whether she was acting or not. This upset Haidee, turning her face red and forcing her to look away. In Leah's eyes this was an admission of guilt.

'Look, I ken yer low on cash,' Leah held up her hands, as if to call a truce- on a battle that Haidee did not wage, 'But I'm no made aw money. If ye can geis half aw it back, I willnae bring it up 'til yer back on yer feet, kay?'

Haidee didn't know what to say at first, and the silence turned Leah's face from concern to anger.

'Dee, fer real! I've given ye ay place tae stay- I buy aw the food- this ain't cool!'

'I didn't take anything.' Haidee said firmly, 'And it fucking hurts that you would think I would!'

'Well, if not you, who?'

'Pete, of course-'

'Oh, aye, blame Pete!' Leah scoffed.

Haidee scoffed right back, 'Yeah, I will blame Pete, a.k.a, the guy who steals all the time!'

'Stole!' Leah pointed her finger, 'He kens better now.'

'Don't defend him, he knew better back then too- and I know you want to believe in him, but I... I'm so...' Tears and sadness broke through her defence, leaving her vulnerable, 'Heartbroken! That you would... Want to believe him over me- when I've stuck by you through all the shit he put you through! And is still putting you through- what the hell happened the other day?'

'Dinnae try fucking twisting things, Dee!' Leah had begun to cry as well, but she would not let it soften her anger, 'He couldnae have taken anything, he's never had the bloody chance!'

'He has a key!'

'No he doesnae!'

Confusion: it appeared on Haidee's face, then spread to Leah's. The cogs in their mind began to turn, similar thoughts appearing in their heads at the same time as if they were telepathic.

'You didn't give him a key?' Haidee spoke first.

'I didnae give him ay key.' Leah let out a long and painful sigh.

'When he came to visit me, he came in on his own, said you gave him a key.'

'Ye didnae tell me that when ye told me he visited.'

'I didn't want to bring it up...' Haidee shrugged, 'I thought... It was a stupid idea to give him a key.'

'Aye, it woulda been. That's why I never gave him ay bloody key.' Leah's voice was rising again, with the level of her anger. Her eyes narrowed down on Haidee.

'Why are you still angry at me?' Haidee asked.

"Cause, ye actually thought I'd give him free access tae ma place.'

'Well I'm pissed off at you!' Haidee snapped, biting the fierce expression right off Leah's face, 'At least I thought you were being naive, not that you were a thief!'

'Well, if ye hadnae thought I wis naive, I wouldnae 'ave thought ye were ay thief!'

Haidee rolled her eyes, 'This isn't right- it's not helping. You shouldn't be angry at me, you should be angry with your brother! He's the one who lied to me and stole from you- and again, I need to ask, what the hell happened the other day?'

'None aw yer bloody business!'

'It is my business! He's affecting our friendship!'

Leah shook her head frantically, 'I ken whit kinda bloke he is, awright? I dinnae expect much from him, but I dae from ye!'

'I haven't done anything!'

'Yer tryna stick yer nose in!'

Haidee finally let go of the duster that she had been clutching this entire unnerving argument, 'I can't win! I honestly can't win! You're just looking for someone to take everything out on 'cause you know your brother is a junkie and always will be!'

The shock was mutual. Even Haidee knew it was a terrible thing to say, and wanted to swallow the words back in. The worst part was that however much she regretted saying it, it was exactly how she felt.

Leah's anger faded into disappointment. She stumbled towards the front door and opened it, gesturing Haidee to go through, 'I need ye tae leave. I need ma space, so... Dinnae come back 'til ye absolutely have tae, 'kay?

Haidee wanted to say no. Being alone was the last thing she needed, but she could see it was what Leah needed. She crammed her feet halfway into her boots, yank her coat off the hook and hobbled out, hearing the door slam behind her. The tears really started to pour, raining down on the doormat, but she covered her mouth so Leah wouldn't hear. After she had adjusted her footwear, put on her coat and taken a few dozen deep breaths, she headed out the building.

It was an aimless wander that led her to Dean Village; a fairytale painting come to life. The hamlet in the heart of Edinburgh was made up of bright and colourful buildings, some dating back to the 12th century. Haidee stood on a bridge, watching how the rare winter sun sprinkled gold upon the river and gave the bare trees a touch of vibrance. The sight brought a sweet aftertaste of summer, but that soon turned sour in her mouth.

'I am *not* in the mood.' she hissed, putting on a hostile demeanor to disguise her fear.

'Will you ever be?' The Watcher appeared in her peripheral vision.

She shrugged, 'We'll see how next year goes.'

'For someone who's been touched by Faith, your outlook is fairly bleak.'

She raised a brow, 'I'm not religious.'

'Never said you were, neither is Faith, or not since he was given his role anyway.'

The comment confused Haidee further but she cottoned on to whom he was speaking about, 'So he... is *Faith*? That man who's like you.'

The Watcher paused, pondering for a moment as he watched the clouds steal the gold out the river. 'We call ourselves Influences, around here anyway. Not sure what it's like up north, or down south, or anywhere else in the world... We can travel fast but not far. We're bound to certain areas.'

'Why?'

He shrugged.

'Well, who put you here? God?'

He shrugged again, 'It depends on what you believe. There's a higher power, yeah, but I really don't know how high it goes, none of us do. We're just given a role and bound to it.'

'So you're just made, plonked down in Edinburgh and don't ask who's boss?'

'No... We were *born*, we were *chosen* in Edinburgh and we ask who's boss but never get an answer.' He put on an ironic grin, 'Then we are bound to our roles indefinitely. Death, Faith, Fear... Hope, Shame and Obsession. All the ingredients to influence the human race.'

His openness was making her wary, making her believe she should close down the conversation, but curiosity prevailed, 'Why are you telling me this?'

'So maybe you'd be a bit more understanding of what I'm doing and why.' He pulled a folded piece of newspaper from his pocket and handed it to her.

Haidee's fingers hovered over the edges of the paper for a moment, as if even taking such a simple thing like a piece of paper from this man would give her a papercut. Eventually, she pinched the corner of it and slid it out of his hand.

Upon unfolding it, she discovered there were a few articles. Politics and environmental issues, mainly, but there was one that stood out. She knew it was the one he wanted her to read. There was a photo of a small child, her grin was wide and smeared with chocolate, dressed in a blue translucent fairy costume, pointing her star-topped wand at the camera. Beside the photo was a headline: *Family Mourns Their Fairy Princess*.

The Watcher did his watching patiently as Haidee's eyes scanned across the page, slowly absorbing the information. After reading it, she lifted her eyes to shoot him a glare.

'Did you do this?' she asked, 'Did you kill her?'

'No!' he shouted, partly from panic and partly from being offended, 'She was hit by a car. She saw other people walking ahead and was excited for the rides she saw across the road. Her mother lost a grip of her hand, and she walked out at the wrong moment.'

'I remember.' she said sadly, 'There's still a memorial at the entrance to the Christmas Market.'

'And her spirit would have stayed there too, if I hadn't passed her on.' He noticed Haidee's glare soften and saw his opportunity to reach her, 'That's what I do. I don't go around killing people, I bring them peace, I move them to the next place. The only time I've taken a living soul was when they were on the brink of death and begged for relief. This circumstance is rare. I don't want to be in this position any more than you do.'

'Then don't. Refuse! Leave me alo-'

'I can't do that.' He shook his head, 'There are far too many consequences, for so many people. There's been too many already.'

'What consequences!' she yelled, her arms spread wide to invite all said consequences to rain down on her, 'Who am I hurting by being here? No one! I'm a good person and I deserve to live! Tell me, tell me one thing that has happened, tell me one *consequence* my life has caused!'

The Watcher became very still and very silent. The trees made more movement and sound than he did as they swayed in the window. A small smile came across Haidee's face as she saw possible victory.

'You can't.' She finally let her arms down, convinced that there were no consequences that would rain on her parade. 'It's all lies, all bullshit. I won't fall for it. You can't name a single reason why I shouldn't be alive-'

'Your mother.'

All hope and the happiness that was growing with it was cut down. Her mind tried to fight the negative thoughts that were intruding, but it failed. In her heart she knew that he was telling the truth, but her conscience needed more.

Each word came out on a sharp breath, 'I-you mean... I dunno what you're saying...'

'You do.'

'No!' She tried to swallow down the certainty, churn it into doubt, 'No, this is another one of your mind games-'

'Haidee.' He took her hand, she was in far too much shock to pull it away, 'What did you think she died of. Stress?'

'Yes! That's- it's an odd explanation but- sometimes they don't always know for sure- bodies are complicated- it's sometimes that simple-'

'No.' He took her other hand and squeezed them both tightly, pulling her frantic gaze away from its aimless journey and straight into his eyes, 'When it can't be explained... We're usually the explanation. I was once human, just like you. I don't remember my life but I had one. I know I was a soldier, and I know I died facing Death straight on, that's why I was given my role, that's why I became an Influence of Death. But other Influences have different ways of coming into their roles. Faith needs someone of pure faith- it doesn't have to be religious- but your mum was, remember?'

'You're saying… I don't understand, she died to become an Influence?'

'No.' He squeezed her hands again, as if his touch was an anchor for her focus, 'Faith wanted her to become an Influence, but if you had died when you were meant to, it would have destroyed her faith. So he put an invisible mark on you that protected you from dying, and made it hard for us other Influences to get to you- and you may think this is a good thing but it had a cost.'

'My mother- you took my mother!' She tried to pull her hands away, he tugged them back towards him.
'I didn't take her, but yes, Death took her as a collateral. It was her life for yours, but it only bought you so much time.' He let go of her hands only to grab hold of her shoulders, 'It has to be you this time Haidee, don't take away someone else's time-'

'Arsehole!' she cried, pushing him off, forcing a parliament of pigeons to take to the skies. 'This isn't me, it's you! You're doing this! You can stop all this- you didn't have to take my mum-'

'There. Are. Consequences.' he spoke in a hushed voice aware that there were now people looking out of their windows, but all they would see is a hysterical young woman screaming at thin air. 'I am begging you to go with me, let me move you on, spare the world any more unnecessary tragedies- at your expense.'

'Stop blaming me, when this is all on you!'

'Do you know how haunted this city is? Do you know how many souls wish they had chosen to be moved on- but had refused? You're just another ghost, Haidee, but the fact you're still in a living breathing body is dangerous!'

'Shut up!'

'If you could see things from my eyes, you'd understand.' The branches of light reappeared from his back, stretching out as much as the width of the ride, casting silver on the water, 'You *will* understand.'

With a flash of light, he was gone.

Haidee was left with her heart in tatters from the damage to her friendship and the revelation of her mother's death.

CHAPTER 16
God Rest Ye Merry, Restless Souls

The top half of Haidee's body flopped over the ledge of the wall. Her hands grasped at the stone whilst her feet made a futile effort to push up the rest of her body. A teenager stubbed out his cigarette and wandered over, holding out for her hand.

'I got you.'

She gratefully grabbed his hand and he pulled her up onto the Folly, Edinburgh's National Monument. It was a structure of twelve pillars, crowning Calton Hill.

She patted herself down and laughed awkwardly, 'It's been a while since I've done this. Thanks.'

'No problem.' He smiled back, then regrouped with his friends who were sharing a chippy while their legs dangled over the edge.

Stepping up beside the impressive Doric pillars, she allowed the view to captivate her, taking her away from the feelings of guilt and anguish. Little black specks wandered up the hill of Arthur's Seat, which was powdered with snow. To the side of this sight, there was a perfect imitation of a rook looming over her: the Nelson Monument.

In the distance, she could see Edinburgh Castle. Dark billowing clouds had broken, just enough, so that the sunset could spray light upon the entire city. She could see all the buses and taxis moving stagnantly through Princes Street, as busy Christmas shoppers were constantly crossing to get to the next store on their list. The clocks of the Balmoral Hotel were already shining their light from the baronial-style building. In its alignment was the Gothic spire of the Walter Scott Monument, covered by the neon colours of the star flyer ride.

Haidee wandered over, passed a couple whose lips dare not be separated and a young tourist who posed for numerous photos, taken by their mother who was standing on the grass, fiddling with technology she didn't quite grasp. She went down the steps onto a small ledge area and allowed her feet to dangle over the edge as she gazed out at the shimmering Firth of Forth.

The Lomond Hills stared back from the Kingdom of Fife, the land on the other side of the water. In the corner of her view, she could see the red-webbed diamonds that created the Forth Rail Bridge, but struggled to see two bridges beyond it for a mist that was descending.

Haidee lay her hands on the slabs beneath her, looking up at the glorious national monument that she sat on. Growing up, she'd never questioned the look of it nor the history of it, believing that they were just put there for their artistry. She never even questioned the nickname of the national monument: the Folly. It was only when her friend Dom became a tour guide that she was given the knowledge of how the grand ornament of Calton Hill came to be.

It was a monument to the fallen Scots of the Napoleonic war. However, every time they put a pillar up they celebrated, spending the funds on grand feasts and ale, drinking away every last penny. Without funding, the project was scrapped, leaving the monument an unfinished folly.

She had always admired it, even then. If anything, that little piece of history gave it some quirkiness. It was still brilliant despite being incomplete, and she wondered if she could be the same.

It was natural to have assumed, up until recently, that she would have seen herself grow old and grey. She spent most of her life learning and working hard, absolved in the idea it would lead her to bigger things. Now she was unemployed, penniless, dependent on her friends and family with no idea of what she wanted to do with her life. There was only one thing she was certain of: she did want to live.

She came to the Folly for nostalgia, for guidance, for hope and, instead, discovered that the fire inside of her, the determination to keep fighting for her life, had calmed into a gentle flame. She allowed herself, for a brief moment, to think of her mum. Little fragments of memories sieved through her mind; her mother's deep-brown hair coiling down her back; the smell of strawberry shampoo and the sparkling earrings that dangled from her ear lobes. She remembered the two of them ice-skating at the Christmas Market and the steam from her homemade leek and potato soup warming her cheeks after a long day of sledging. She could remember feeling care-free, falling asleep between her parents while watching *Home Alone*.

The absence of her mother was a pain that was too strong, she had decided to put all memories of her on a shelf within her mind. The clips she played in her mind were dusty and damaged, all she could manage to see was seconds of each moment. All she had were little clues to find the mother she had lost.

What she needed to do was to remember her well enough to know what advice she would have given. It was impossible. What she remembered was all she could remember, snippets of a wonderful woman she loved, a woman that had been gone for nearly two decades. Now, all she had left from her mother was the life that Death wanted to snuff out.

If not for herself, then she would keep on fighting for her mum. She wouldn't be a folly, incomplete, half-done. She had to make a life for herself, for her mother.

Fuel to the fire; she was burning bright again.

In the six o'clock winter darkness, she made her way down the steps and walked in the direction of the main city, heading home to Leah. In her head, she was rehearsing the apology she would give, proof-reading every line, making sure to take responsibility for the hurt she had caused. The street had a few people making their way back and forth from the centre, yet, even while she was preoccupied by her silent recital, she was the only one who noticed a small girl in a party dress walk through the gates of Old Calton Cemetery.

Haidee slowed down as she walked by, watching the little girl skip up the steps unaccompanied.

She turned to a woman who was leaning against the wall, texting on her phone.

'Is she your kid?' she asked.

The woman looked confused, shook her head and continued to hit the screen with her thumbs. At this point, Haidee was done with graveyards. They held unnerving memories and they were exactly where her Watcher wanted her to be. It would be moronic to go in.

'Hey there!' she shouted into the darkness, 'You shouldn't be playing in here, you can get hurt or locked in!'

There was no reply. She had made up her mind to leave but her feet were bound by morality to stay. The little girl's parents didn't seem to be about and a pitch-black graveyard was nowhere for a child to play in. If she left, only to see the girl's face on the news the next day, missing, abducted or dead, she wouldn't be able to forgive herself.

Begrudgingly, Haidee tiptoed up the steps in pursuit of the little girl. There were a few streetlamps dimly lighting the cemetery, she used the torch on her phone to push away the shadows that remained.

'Please, don't jump out!' she warned, for her own safety. 'I can't leave you in here, you'll trip up or... A bad man might get you. Can you please just come out?'

The little girl would not respond. Haidee's instincts told her once more to leave, that the caretaker would surely find the little girl and that it was not her responsibility. It was a tempting idea to give into, especially as the eerie surroundings were giving her chills, but her conscience would not permit her to abandon the silly child.

The torch light caught the girl- barefoot on stone- Haidee jumped at the sight of her but as her brain processed what she was seeing, it told Haidee that this was not the little girl. What she was looking at was a statue. It was turquoise and in the shape of a man, reaching up towards another statue: Abraham Lincoln. It was a memorial statue to Scottish-American soldiers who died in America's civil war. She circled the statue, but there was still no sign of the child.

An unnerving thought crossed Haidee's mind: she may have just walked into another mind game. That thought was enough to make her abandon the pleas of her conscience and walked right out the graveyard- then she heard it. A giggle and a scuffle at the back of the cemetery. It came from one of the mausoleums. They were tiny gateless houses with no roofs, yet, they had decorated grand doorways that presented the areas as manors of the dead.

'Please, I can hear you, come on- your parents will be worried!'

Still, no word from the little girl and no noise followed. Frustration had trumped fear, Haidee huffed before popping her head into each ghostly house. Then, fear had trumped all.

Her phone slipped from her hand, just as her nerves had slipped from her control. Her mouth opened instinctively, ready to let out the cry that was already rising from her chest. Seeing one finger placed against its lips, she obeyed the request for silence and the scream dissolved in her throat.

In front of her eyes stood the girl, whom she now wished she had never followed. This wasn't a girl at all, not anymore. The phone had landed at an angle, directing the light into the corner of the mausoleum. Where the light caught the little girl, she appeared as real and alive as Haidee was. However, where the light failed to touch, she didn't exist. Her left arm and ear had been devoured by shadows.

A smile spread across the little girl's lips. A sound of moaning metal cured Haidee of her paralysed state, she turned to see the gate had closed. She ran towards it, mumbling the word "no" over and over, as if it were a password to reopen the gate. She slammed against the bars, rattling them and calling out for help. There was no one on her side of the street, not even at the bus stop- but there was a group of young adults walking on the opposite side. She screamed for their help but all they offered her was laughter and unhelpful drunken comments.

She had to call for help, she had to call Leah. A grim realisation took hold when she reached in her pocket for her phone: she had left it in the mausoleum. It was a horrid scenario to play her mind through, turning to face that ghost, willingly walking towards it. There was no getting around it. She was trapped, and her key out of there was with the dead.

The first steps were stumbles back up the stairs, after that it was simple enough. In an attempt to distract herself, she focused on her own panting and the warm clouds of breath coming from her mouth, immediately slain by the winter air. She was halfway there when she felt as though she had hit an ice wall. The raw coldness soaked through every layer she was wearing and even through her skin.

She whimpered, telling herself that it was not what she already knew it to be. The sensation had touched the bottom of her heels to the top of her scalp. It was too tall to be the little girl. It was another ghost.

Melting the cold feeling on her back was the fire inside her. Determination, fed by anger and frustration, flared inside her. This was a game Death had already played with her and she had won the last round. If Death could do no harm to her, then neither could the dead.

As hesitant as her fear was to leave, she managed to push it aside, just enough to turn around. It was a man who was pressed against her, with bulging eyes highlighted by the glow that skimmed over her head. Where his jaw should be, was a gaping hole instead, but she could tell that this man was not smiling. Neither was she.

She needed one word, just one word, to tell this creature that she was not afraid. A word of defiance, of rebellion, of bravery.

'Boo.' Was the word.

Hearing this, the ghost became enraged and flew through Haidee's body, drowning her in the icy sensation. With her heart in a tantrum, she dashed towards the mausoleum, noticing the graveyard was filled with shadow-bitten specters. They wailed and thrashed against her, each boltic ache became more overwhelming that the last, dragging her down to her knees.

She refused to scream, she could not give her Watcher the satisfaction, but even with all her experience of broken bones, pneumonia and food poisoning, she had never felt pain like this. It was severing her nerves, burrowing deep into her bones and burning through her veins.

The scream could only be prevented one way. She stuck the length of her thumb between her teeth, groaning as the torment forced her teeth through the fabric of her glove and her skin. The crunching of bone could be felt as she tasted the blood that filled her mouth.

Seeing through the slits of her clenched eyes that the phone was in reach, she dragged it towards her with her fingertips until she could grasp it in her hand. Miraculously, the phone was still unlocked. Leah was on the home page as a favourite contact, two prods from Haidee's finger and the phone began to ring. The sound warned away the ghosts, causing them to withdraw to the edges of the graveyard. The pain immediately relinquished, with the exception of her bleeding thumb. She spat out the blood as the call connected.

'I'm stuck in Calton Cemetery!' Haidee yelled down the speaker before Leah had the chance to speak.

A voice answered, but it wasn't Leah. The automated voice of the answering machine spoke its usual spiel, giving the ghosts permission to swoop down upon Haidee.

She quickly redialed, but she couldn't stop them from pushing their way through her, draining her of all warmth and relief. The ringing pushed them back a second time, but only for a brief moment as it went immediately to voicemail. It was clear Leah was intent on not picking up. Haidee tried a third, then a fourth, then a fifth time- all the while being attacked by the restless souls of Edinburgh.

Finally, Leah answered, 'Can ye no take ay hint! I dinnae wanna talk-'

She could hear Haidee's whimpers down the phone, which was all she was capable of as the ghosts kept her frozen in pain.

'Dee, whit's wrong?'

'I-I'm stuck... Calton...' She squeezed her eyes shut, putting all her focus on the knowledge that Leah was on the other side of the phone, 'I'm stuck in Calton Cemetery, help me!'

'How can ye be stuck?'

'L-locked in.' The pain was beginning to restrict the movement of her chest, air would leave her lungs quicker than it had entered.

'Dee, ye having a panic attack?'
'Yes!' She lied, gladly taking the realistic explanation handed to her, 'I need you! I'm sorry, please!'

'Awright- dinnae freak out, yer lucky I'm ten minutes away.'

'Please, hurry!'

'On ma way!' She hung up.

The relief was short-lived. Leah didn't have a key to the cemetery, but knowing her friend was coming to her aid gave her the last bit of fight she needed.

She pushed herself up from the ground and ran towards the gate, breaking through the pain-inflicting silhouettes. There were at least eighteen ghosts standing between her and the outside world. They stood in garments she recognised from history books and period dramas, bulbous petticoats and cravat ties.

An idea, as hopelessly hopeful as it was, presented itself as the only possible form of escape. With the help of a gravestone, she could climb the wall.

She bolted towards the corner of the cemetery, trying to avoid the aisle of ghouls waiting for her. They were on her heels, hastening after her, but her desperation pushed her past her limit, reaching a speed she had never achieved in her entire life. The only chance they had to catch up to her is when she had to stop running and start climbing.

They hunted her down, clawing at her with their icy nails. The pain impared her ability to keep a steady balance on the gravestone nearest the wall. She slipped time and time again, battering her knees, shins and chin against the stone. No injury could stop her from trying again. There was no giving up.

It took all her strength to push through the agony they had inflicted upon her but, for a few seconds, she managed to. Her foot pushed down hard on the very top of the gravestone, it shifted with her weight. She lunged against the wall, throwing her torso over and scrambling up.

Considering the two people below, she shouted 'Move!' Before gripping onto the ledge and sliding her body down the wall.

'Dee!' Leah squelled, running towards her.

The two people were watching eagerly, almost enjoying the spontaneity that was added to their evening. Leah stood directly under.

'You absolute nutjob!' Her eyes flared with worry.

'Out the way!' Haidee shouted down to her, feeling her grip loosening.

'I'll catch you!' Leah insisted, rolling up her sleeves and spreading out her arms, 'Or else you'll break something!'

'I'll break you if you don't move!'
'Dinnae worry 'bout–'

Haidee had lost her grip.

A scream. Leah's scream. It was so full of heartbreak that Haidee didn't want to open her eyes, in case she saw herself on the ground, dead. Then she felt a nudge on the shoulder.

'You mad woman! Why would you do that?' Leah's voice was a mixture of rage, fear and affection, as if she was the parent and Haidee was her child.

'It was the only way out.' Haidee groaned, her entire body shaking but intact.

She turned and examined herself. Her clothes were a state, bloodied and torn at the knee. A blanket of numbness covered her arms and legs. She reviewed her last memory, the ground had rushed to meet her but she covered her face with crossed arms and took the shock of the impact through her feet. Then, the force sprawled her across the pavement. The concrete had kissed the side of her face, leaving a scratch.

Leah helped to slowly raise her from the ground, then brought her over to sit at the bus stop. After she made sure Haidee wasn't in need of an ambulance, she went to inspect the gate. Haidee's heart sank as she heard its metal moan again.

'It wasnae even bloody locked, ye numpty!' Leah stormed over, 'I thought that! They don't even close this one, the ghost tours pass through here!'

'But I tried to open it...' Haidee murmured, struggling to process her trauma.

"Clearly no hard enough!' She inspected Haidee's palms that had been cut on the ledge, 'Yev made ay right mess aw yersel.'

The people at the bus stop were whispering to each other as they continued to watch Haidee's live show with interest.

Leah took notice of this and helped Haidee to walk, 'Ye guid enough tae walk hame?'

Haidee nodded, too bewildered to speak anymore.

'Whit were ye daeing in there, anyway?'

She concentrated on her breathing for a few minutes and Leah waited patiently for an answer.

She finally admitted, 'I followed a little girl in.'

'Aw, well I didnae see her jump over the flaming wall.'

'Well...' Haidee didn't know how else to put it, 'She wasn't really there...'

Leah simpered, 'Yer first ghost experience, eh? Well, ye've lived in Edinburgh long enough. Bound tae happen eventually.'

'I was in a coma for five days, it's probably just brain issues...'

'Maybe not. Maybe the gate wis locked. Maybe the wee ghosty girl locked ye in!'

Haidee laughed loudly with Leah in an attempt to seem normal. Truthfully, she believed her friend had hit the nail on the head.

CHAPTER 17
I Wonder As I Wander

'We need to talk about this.' Leah said, the solemnity of her tone was an unusual fit for her personality.

She had taken over rebandaging Haidee's hands, after noticing Haidee was struggling to do so herself. Matthew watched in quiet concern. They were in a quirky little cafe not far from his workplace, it was his lunch break.

'I don't feel right about leaving you over Christmas.' she continued, 'I'd feel better if you went with your dad.'

Haidee had lied to her dad and told him that she would be spending Christmas with Leah's family in North Queensferry, a village north of the Firth of Forth. If Leah could invite her, she would, the issue was space. Leah's modest four-bedroom home was expected to hold her, her parents, her three brothers, their significant others and all the children.

'I'll be fine.' Haidee didn't protest the idea of spending her Christmas with her dad, or even Moira; it was Moira's entire family she had an objection to.

Even ghosts couldn't spook her into going, and neither could Leah's heavy stare.

'Is there naeb'dy?' Leah said, 'Can't yer grandparents pay yer flight over tae Spain, tae spend ay Christmas with their lovely granddaughter?'

'I barely talk to them.' Haidee laughed to cover up the sad fact of the situation, 'Even if they had the money to get me there... It would be the same as spending Christmas with Moira's family. I just don't want to be an add on to someone else's celebration.'

'But it's better than fuck aw! Ye jamp aff ay wall the size af ay hoose 'cause ye didnae realise the bloody gate wis open! I really dinnae feel comfortable leaving ye tae go tae work as it is. I'm scared fer ye.'

Haidee had never witnessed Leah look helpless before and it was a hard sight to bear. She didn't want to be a burden to anyone she cared about.

'We have plans.' Haidee smiled towards Matthew, trying to reassure Leah, 'I've been looking forward to this since Matt got me the tickets last Christmas. I haven't been to a Christmas Eve ceilidh since my mum was alive, I'm not missing this. So it's just one day alone. Just Christmas, and I'll see you on Boxing Day.'

'But it's not just Christmas...' Matthew finally spoke up, although there was clear hesitation in his voice, 'We think... maybe you should go live with your dad for a while.'

'What?' It was a surprise for only her, as she turned to Leah it became apparent that this had already been discussed between her two friends.

'It's no that I dinnae want ye livin' with me or that,' Leah was quick to console her, 'But yer no daeing guid, hun. Ye refuse tae go on universal credit, ye canny find ay job- yer physical an' mental health have gone tae shit...'

'You're acting differently too.' Matthew added, taking her hand to make sure she knew that they were on her side, 'You used to be calm and laid back, always looking on the bright side, always helping people find the best solutions- Now you don't even try to figure out a solution for yourself. It's like all the positivity has been drained out of you.'

For the briefest of moments, Haidee considered telling them everything. Maybe her two realist, agnostic friends would be open-minded to the existence of a messenger of Death. Matthew heavily relied on scientific proof, so he would immediately call her sanity into question. She wouldn't blame him for doing so, since she did the same thing many times. Leah was a little more welcoming to the unknown; she based many relationship decisions on her daily horoscope and was convinced her aunt's house was haunted, but her belief in these things seemed like a half-hearted amusement.

She was just playing pretend, and unfortunately, Haidee's game had very real stakes.

Matthew continued, 'I've talked to my sister, she's happy to drop you off in Stirling with all your things, on our way to Fort William. We can leave the ceilidh about eleven, you'll be there for midnight.' At that, the sound of a foghorn wailing over and over again interrupted every conversation in the cafe. He scrambled at his pockets, yanking out his phone and silencing the boisterous sound. 'That's my cue, duty calls.'

'I've gotta head back too.' Leah groaned, rolling her eyes, 'It's stock day. Lot's ay counting, yay.'

'Just think about it, Dee.' Matthew squeezed Haidee's shoulder, 'Please.'

'We can talk about it more when I get hame tonight.' Leah added.

Haidee kept wearing her soft smile, covering the insecurity she felt in her little unemployed bubble. Her friends left, waving energetically as they went out to win their bread. The empty plates and glasses kept her company for a few seconds before a waitress took them away. It was clearly time for her to leave too, having no reason to stay, and she did so with great reluctance.

Only two o'clock in the afternoon but it was already getting dark. Thick black clouds had blocked out the sun and lay down on the city, creating a mist that erased the horizon. There was no wind, which was rare in Edinburgh, but it was eerily quiet and colder than usual.

Haidee turned onto the Royal Mile where she could only see metres ahead of her. Shapes of buildings hid within the fog and, further on, some had even been engulfed entirely by the grey.

People faded in and out of her sights as she walked through the mist. On the walk to the cafe, she had kept her eyes on Leah the entire time and managed to distract herself from her surroundings. Now, she was alone and she had to face what the fog would not hide.

The Royal Mile had never seemed more crowded than when the dead occupied it. All their eyes were on her. It was impossible to keep her head down. The ghosts were not only a threat but acted as obstacles, preventing her from seeing the people on the other side of each specter. After nearly bumping into a few frustrated people, she managed to get the hang of it. Feeling confident, she quickened her pace.

Staying near all the buildings, she saw a clear path ahead of her and charged on. Then, out of the wall, an apparition of a Victorian woman blocked her. Her feet slammed on the breaks, and quickly reversed their movements. Suddenly, she was launched into the ghost's ice-cold form and froze while their beings overlapped.

'Watch it!' croaked the middle-aged woman who had barged into her, not having the time to stop as quickly as Haidee had.

Haidee couldn't say anything as the woman walked by her. She was soaking in bitter coldness and more than a century of someone else's misery. It took her a moment to push through the shock of the sensation, but as soon as she did, her feet led her away, pulling her out of the apparition.

She looked over her shoulder to see the ghost still staring at her, but she didn't hunt her down like the ones in the graveyard. All she did was stare at her with large sad eyes, before turning away and heading to the Royal Mile.

It was starting to dawn on Haidee that the ghosts were not going to harm her this time, not intentionally. She wondered what was different this time; was it the time of day? Was it that she wasn't alone this time? Was it that the cemetery had been their domain, and she had trespassed on it? Whatever the answer, she was relieved that she could walk through her city without being hunted.

For now.

Cogs in her mind began to turn. Perhaps the ghosts she came across were bad people, and therefore bad spirits. Maybe, generally speaking, most ghosts were just going about their afterlife with no ill intentions. A door opened in her thoughts, letting hope in through the gap. Maybe her mother could still be around.

If so there was one place she was likely to be. It was a special place for her and her parents; a place for family picnics, celebratory ice cream and an escape when times got rough. That is where Matilda McLean was put to rest. Her ashes were spread across a bed of lavender.

Haidee turned back and headed in the direction of the almost-secret garden that lay hidden in the Old Town area of Edinburgh. The fog drained all the colour from the city, and with the century-old buildings creeping out from beneath the veil of mist, it felt to Haidee as though she was stepping into the past.

It was hard to tell the living from the dead as it was without a statue thrown into the mix, but the bronze figure of an 18th-century Scottish poet was her marker to take the next left. She dived into Dunbar's Close, narrowly avoiding an entity whose lower half was gnawed off by shadows.

The haze spared the garden and only surrounded it with white beyond its walls. It was bright enough to give it a heavenly glow, bringing out the vibrancy of the flowers that refused to wilt at winter's will.

'Mum?' she called, scaring a few birds into flight.

There was no answer.

She walked further into the garden, peering through the trellis to watch for movement, scoping the lawn for phantoms. On a stone bench by the wall, she took a seat right opposite the bed of lavender.

'Mum?' She tried once more.

The reply did not come in the form of a word but visually: there he was.

Her Watcher stood on the other side of the flower bed, his branches of light faded out quickly against the misty background. Being watched had become a feeling too familiar now, like air in the lungs: it was just a way of life.

The disappointment was a dull ache, her hopes weren't high enough for the fall to break her.

'It was worth a try.' she sighed, 'I just thought I'd try.'

'You should be relieved, she's moved on.' He tried to reassure her, 'If she'd waited here, she wouldn't be the same. Just a sad auld creature.'

'Like me?'

'That's no what I said.'

'But that's why you sent the ghosts after me right? To scare me into not wanting to end up like them?'

'I didn't *send* them after you, they've always been here. I just allowed you to see through my eyes, see that there is a fate worse than death. I didn't expect you to wander into a graveyard.'

'So you saw that and did nothing?' She laughed bittersweetly. A victory point, proving him a monster, but she was pained that her suffering had an audience.

'I wasn't with you then. I thought I'd give you some space. I thought you'd ask for me if you needed me-'

'Ask for you?' She looked aghast, 'Why the hell would I ask for you?'

'Because I want to help you.'

'By torturing me, by messing with my head, by making me haunted-'

'I'm not trying- that's not what I want- Haidee-'

'Forget it!' She lunged from her seat, ready to charge away, 'None of it will work anyway, you'll never get your wa-'

The gasp was shrill. The air swept into her lungs so suddenly, that she forgot how to exhale. Her breath was suspended, as well as the pain, but only momentarily. The minute she breathed out, gravity dragged her to the floor.

She felt her Watcher's hands on her, and instantly believed he was to blame, until she saw his face. As he turned her towards him, she could see his brows stitched together with concern.

'Haidee…' He hovered his hands over different areas of her body, lingering over the parts where the pain was strongest, wincing as though he could feel it himself, 'Haidee, what the hell happened?'

She had no idea. Turning her head, she glimpsed the purple of the lavender, before the pain blinded all her senses.

The scream was not a plea for help, but the voice of the pain itself.

CHAPTER 18

HALLELUJAH

Death lingered like a vulture, closer than he ever did before. The Watcher watched over her as she stared back up. The drugs muffled the pain, but her nerves were still shrieking, begging for mercy.

Haidee knew there was something terribly wrong, the agony was beyond anything she had ever felt. Her body had become a car on fire, ready to explode, and her soul was trapped inside.

It was impossible for her to concentrate on what the doctors were saying as they tended to her, but her ears grasped at enough words for her to understand.

"Miracle."
"Internal bleeding."
"Multiple fractures."
"Possible ruptured aorta."
"It's like she fell off a building."
"How is she still alive?"

The doctors wouldn't understand that the drugs wouldn't work on her. The torments of her invisible wounds were bound in her flesh. The introduction of the scalpel could be felt, its sharpness carving into her, worsening her misery.

She could no longer scream. There were two choices: lie there on the operating table, paralysed, enduring an unendurable pain, or...

'Take my hand.' The Watcher reached his hand between the doctors, they didn't take notice. 'Nobody is meant to be in this much pain. Haidee, you don't deserve to be in this much pain.'

There was a part of her that wanted to, that needed to, but the pain held her arm down.

'The minute you decide to take my hand,' he continued, 'That'll be it, you'll be out of your body, you'll be safe.'

There was desperation, there was willingness to give up, to give in. There was surrender. Still, her hand would not move.

His fingers sprawled out in front of her, begging to intertwine with hers, 'Let me help you!'

There was no comprehension of what he had just said. Her world no longer consisted of words, shapes, colours and sounds. There was just feeling, *one* feeling: agony.

The Watcher looked down at her, like a helpless and lost child. Collateral damage of a battle between Influences.

Faith was nowhere to be seen, abandoning the life he claimed to save. If he would not relent, then The Watcher would.

He lowered his hand on her chest, feeling the pulse of her heart in the palm of his hand. Her mind slipped away into a dream while the pain left her body. As the surgeon sliced into her chest, they discovered no damage. Every rib was intact. Her lung had no puncture wound. The bones in her left arm, leg and hip were perfectly fine.

The doctors looked to each other for answers, which they would never get.

Every member of the hospital's staff were astonished when Haidee walked out of the building two hours later. With no ailment to speak of, she was discharged shortly after she woke up and announced she felt fine. The doctors recommended testing, but no test was required for her to know what happened. They asked for her details, at least, as she hadn't been carrying any identification. She hadn't had her wallet on her, since the lunch was Matthew's treat. That little serendipity meant that her father hadn't been contacted, nor Leah, nor anyone else. Her trip to hospital would be a secret between her and Death's messenger.

The walk to Leah's from the Royal Infirmary was long, but her body had more energy than it had since she was a child. The mist was clearing just as the sun was setting, giving her a light to guide her home. There were no ghosts on her journey, or at least, none that she could see. The nagging feeling hadn't been tugging at her neck, but at her side the entire walk home. She had given him enough space, knowing full well he was walking by her side.

The journey gave her time to reflect on what just happened and why. The Watcher would not appear to say he told her so, but she did remember him telling her so: *If you got hit by a train, you'd break every bone in your body, fracture your skull and have your muscles torn apart, but you'd still survive.* The wall of Calton Cemetery was as high as a house. The adrenaline must have masked the pain until it left her system.

At the crossroads of Inverleith park, she looked to the void that begged her instincts for attention.

'Thank you.' she said, 'I don't know why you did it, but thank you.'

He didn't show himself but The Watcher was there, staring right back at her, unable to say a word.

'I know you weren't supposed to do that.' She became tearful. Hatred and gratitude battled inside her, overwhelming her and challenging all that she knew. 'I know that tomorrow might be a different story... But you saved me today, so thank you.'

She continued on, but he stayed put. After several steps ahead, she stopped, feeling his stare now on her back. She knew what he was doing. Looking over her shoulder, she smiled and nodded to him, even though he still remained invisible to her.

He examined her smile for a moment, taking a mental photograph, capturing the orange glow from the sunset setting the world aflame as this living woman showed him a mercy he never thought he'd be so lucky to receive: gratitude and forgiveness.

When he turned away, she felt the burden of his stare lifted. An unspoken truce had been made, and she knew she had to enjoy it while it lasted.

CHAPTER 19
All I Want For Christmas

There were six hours and twenty-five minutes left of Christmas Eve. Haidee had sent numerous texts to Matthew asking if the plan was still the same. He didn't reply, presumably because he was getting ready, so she assumed the plan was as discussed: meet on The Mound, walk to The Hub together.

Leah insisted that she borrow her lucky high heels; judging by their appearance, the luck it bestowed on the wearer was the miracle of not breaking an ankle. Upon touching them, they bestowed Haidee with a different luck: the luck of finding Leah's three-year-old small-heeled pixie boots at the back of the wardrobe. Lady Luck would give her feet a comfortable evening, that was the least she could offer.

Haidee's coat covered all but an inch of her dress and kept her top half well-heated. However, there was nothing but thin nylon between her legs and the harsh bite of the frosty air forced her usual pace to triple. It had only been two minutes since she left the flat when it started snowing.

As she neared her destination, she felt a buzz from her pocket, but only because her fingertips brushed against it. Her legs moved at such a pace that the buzzing felt like the brushing of fabric against her thigh. When she pulled out her phone, she saw Matthew's name on the screen. She declined; there was no point answering since she would see him momentarily. Then she noticed she had four other missed calls from him. The phone rang again in her hand as she was reaching the top of The Mound. Cafe Musa was just around the corner, along with Matthew. His phone was pressed to his ear and a large backpack sat by his side.

Waiting for a car to pass, she shouted over to him, 'You won't be able to sneak food in, not with that!'

He gave a half-smile and cancelled his call. She walked over to him, feeling uneasy at his less-than-enthusiastic welcome. Her stomach tangled itself, preparing for disappointment. The backpack was too obvious a clue as to what he would say next.

'I'm so sorry Haidee,' he opened his arms to her, 'the snow's getting heavier, my sister wants to get going now, we gotta get home.'

She hugged him and tried to muffle her sigh, 'I understand, you look so cool too.' She pulled back and admired the reds, greens, blues and yellows of his kilt.

'And you look stunning!' He gestured to her hair, half up with spring in her curls. He pulled out the entry tickets for the ceilidh and gave them to her, 'You'll have a wonderful time.'

'I can't go alone! I need a partner to dance with.'

'All you need to do is use your charm and you'll have a queue of partners lining up.' He beamed at her squeezing her arms.

She hit him playfully, 'You're dangerously smooth.'

A car pulled up into the carpark next to them, Matthew watched it with sad eyes as he did.

He pulled her into another hug, 'That's Maria here, but if you're not going to the ceilidh then please reconsider the other offer, we can drop you off at your dad's?'

'I'm happy in Edinburgh.'

'Then you need to go to the ceilidh, it'd break my heart to know you're spending Christmas alone.'

'I enjoy my own company, I'm great company.'

'Agreed, that's why you should give all these people waiting at the ceilidh some company, in the spirit of Christmas, give a little!'

'*Smooth.*'

'Please, please, please-'

'I'll go to the ceilidh.' She pulled back with a smile on her face, 'I'm all dressed up, you bought the tickets, it'd be a shame to waste it.'

Satisfied with what his haggling had achieved, he was comfortable with saying his farewell. Haidee waved him goodbye as she watched him and his sister drive off.

She took a seat on the brick wall, feeling sorry for herself as snowflakes fluttered down beside her. As much as she did not want to go alone, she was stupidly charmed into a promise. Knowing Matthew, he would want a detailed account of the night with a few photos as evidence. It was hard to face the dread when an even more dreadful thing was watching her.

'What's worse than sitting here pitying myself, is that you're watching me while I'm doing it.' She glared over to a seemingly-empty area of street, sensing his presence so strongly, she didn't need to see him, 'What's the point hiding anymore? You know I can tell.'

He appeared within a blink, looking rather embarrassed, 'Well... You had company and some bad news.'

'I've had worse news.' Such as: she was meant to be dead and she needed to die.

Cautiously, he took a seat beside her, watching her change of expression to see if it bothered her or not. It did not.
'What's on today's agenda?'

He didn't answer. She waited, looking at him expectantly until she realised, he didn't have an answer.

'Why are you here?'

Again, no answers. They sat together in silence, watching the snow lay down a thin blanket of white in front of them. There was no fear of him anymore, no anger or hatred. What she felt was strange and unusual to her, a cross between pity and hope for him. It was clear by his face that he was tired and defeated, not from anything she had done, but by being weighed down by his own conscience.

Her question was asked quietly, as she was unsure whether or not she really wanted to ask it, 'Can you dance?' He was stunned but after she had said it, she spoke more confidently, trying to convince herself that this was a good idea, 'I'm assuming you're free?'

He sat upright, unable to do anything but stare at her and, with that stare, demanded an explanation.

'I was thinking about that story, that true story, you know, about World War I. The British and the German soldiers, who had been shooting at each other only moments before, managed to find a way to celebrate Christmas with each other. Singing, playing football, even exchanging gifts with things they had on them, even though they knew they'd have to shoot at each other the next day. They'd have to kill each other the next day.' She pressed her stare against him until he looked her in the eyes, 'I'm suggesting a truce.'

'I'm not your enemy.'

'You want me dead.'

'I don't want you dead.' he said with all sincerity, 'This isn't about what I want.'

'If it was... What would you want?'

Silence fell upon them as cold and gently as the snow. It was clear to her that this was the first time The Watcher thought about what he wanted. Her reckless imagination put herself into his shoes, overwhelming her with the burden of his necessary evil. She thought over everything he had done, forcing her into a coma, threatening her, terrifying her. He also created a wholesome world for her, reached out to her to try and make her understand, and also showed mercy when he could have let her suffer and beg for death. They were more alike than she wanted to admit to herself. Both conflicted. Both tired and defeated. Truthfully, she didn't want a truce, she wanted peace.

'I want to dance with you.' He finally broke the silence, 'I want a truce, I would... really, *really* like that.'

For the first time, they exchanged smiles. He removed his haggard jumper, revealing a fairly nice shirt that could pass for formal. He offered his arm to her, and she took it. It surprised her how warm she felt, and how comfortable she was with his hand on hers.

Her instincts told her that she was safe, and that the decision she had made was good for both of them.

However, there was a little voice of doubt that spoke logically. It said: this man is a threat to your life.

Haidee was about to dance with the devil.

CHAPTER 20
Fairytale of Edinburgh

The ballroom was breathtaking. The wooden structures appeared gold against the rich blue of the walls and curtains which were decorated with triangular patterns. Lights were twisted around the railings of the gallery, twinkling like fireflies around the whole room.

There were small square tables acting as a barrier between chairs and the dancing area around the edge of the grand room. Two longer rectangular tables indicated that that was where the buffet would be presented later on. Most of the tables were already claimed.

A band was setting up. Thankfully, there was not an accordion player in sight, which meant that they wouldn't have to skip along to the tedious melodies that were forced upon Haidee when she did Scottish country dancing in primary school; played from a decade-old cassette.

As they scoped the dance hall for seats, The Watcher felt the tables turn, now he was being watched. It was only for seconds at a time, the odd glance in his directions. He had made himself visible to all, which he didn't do too often, as he rarely needed to. When he did, it was always a nerve-racking experience, but this time he felt far more comfortable. This time, he wasn't alone.

Haidee asked an old couple if the seat next to them was available, which it was, and claimed it with her belongings, as well as The Watcher's coat and tattered jumper. The old woman awed at her and complimented her dress. It was maroon with a modest bateau neckline and velvet floral decal cascaded from the shoulders all the way down to the edges of her flared skirt.

'It's a hand-me-down.' She smiled awkwardly, always unsure of how to respond to compliments.

The hostess walked to the front of the stage as the seven-piece band stood at the ready. She welcomed everyone to the charity ceilidh, explaining that all the proceeds from the tickets would go to Fresh Start. She then went into detail about what Fresh Start did and the help they provided to previously-homeless people settling into their new homes. She encouraged people to donate throughout the night, pointing to a woman she called Linda who stood at the back of the ballroom, wearing a silly Christmas jumper, reindeer antlers and a cheerful grin while holding a donations bucket.

The woman then introduced the band and announced the buffet would be at eight o'clock. Finally, she asked people to partner up and then form a group of five partners, declaring that the first dance would be The Gypsy's Thread.

The old couple immediately invited them to form a group and together they found another group of six people, a family mixed of parents and kids, to complete the set. The partners stood opposite each other, but Haidee grasped her Watcher's hand preventing him from doing the same.

She whispered to him, 'Before we do this, I think you owe me your real name.'

He was about to answer when the hostess started loudly going over the steps of the dance. He quickly backed into his position, leaving Haidee to stare on expectantly.

A long held note sounded on the fiddle, leading the other instruments into the song. They were at the head of the group, which meant they had to take the lead. They took the hands of the people beside them and everyone else held hands to form a U-shape.

At the first beat, her Watcher and the old man had formed an arch which Haidee led the chain through, eventually causing them to twirl against each other to unknot the chain. The same was repeated, only this time with her Watcher leading the chain under her and the old woman's arms.

With hands free, the partners then orbited each other back-to-back. At this point, her Watcher said something, a three-syllable word, that she didn't quite catch. They then returned to their original positions.

Partners then spun, holding each other's right hands. Haidee made sure to pull him close, 'I didn't catch that.'

The rest of the partners went back into position whilst Haidee and her Watcher joined their left hands together as well and burled down the aisle.

'That's my name.' he said, 'Corstorphine.'

They let go of each other and assumed their places at the tail of the group. They then took hands again, along with the people beside them and the dance started again.

Haidee was familiar with the area of Edinburgh called Corstorphine. She had only ever been to visit Edinburgh Zoo. Yet, she had never known anyone with that name, first or last. It didn't exactly roll off the tongue.

After the dance was finished, the hostess immediately prepared them for another one. In the space of an hour they had done The Gypsy Thread, Strip The Willow, Dashing White Sergeant, The Postie's Jig, The Eightsome Reel and The Britannia Two-Step. Each dance required a different amount of partners, morphing the group and even moving them to a new one at a point. The Britannia Two-Step relieved Haidee of Corstorphine for a dance as it required three people. She joined with two of the children of their first group and he joined the elderly couple. The old woman was more than smitten, with her husband in one hand and a young man in the other.

To the reprieve of tired feet attached to sweaty bodies, the hostess announced the buffet and a break from all the jigging. The band lay down their instruments and Christmas tunes began belting through the speakers. The children, with their unlimited supply of energy, continued to dance away and play football with some of the balloons scattered about.

Haidee and Corstorphine practically raced to the buffet table, desperate for water and anything that could replenish their spirit. She took a look at his plate, amused by the pyramid of sausage rolls he created. He found her own selection funny; cakes balancing on top of each other on one side, away from the pile of Pringles upon a handful of cocktail sausages upon a heap of salad.

Haidee suggested they eat up in the gallery, taking their belongings with them. They slotted their plates in the wooden ledge under the twinkling railings and ate together, too exhausted to overthink their situation.

'So... *Corstorphine*...' Haidee couldn't help but giggle as she said it, 'Is that your full name?'

'It's what I got called.' He shrugged, 'It's all we remember when we take on our roles. When I started there were two others. Arthur and Estonia. We just remember a place, dunno if it's where we're from, or an important place to us. Arthur just remembered Arthur's

Seat and used to hang around there all the time- said he felt something. I never feel anything in Corstorphine.'

'Well it's a bit of a mouthful, Corstorphine.'

'Well, you're the only person who seems to require a name for me, so what's easiest for you?'

'You want me to name you?'

'Aye. Why no?'

She began to ponder as she stuffed several cocktail sausages into her mouth, licking the grease off her fingers. 'Well it makes sense to give you a nickname based on that, so... Cory?'

'No.'

'Phinnie?'

'No.'

'Well, Tory then, you definitely *act* like you're a Tory.' She smirked.

He raised his brows, pleasantly surprised by her cheekiness, 'You cheeky wee bisom.'

'*Bisom*? Okay, grampa.'

'Oi, don't disrespect your elders.'

She paused for a second, examining the features of his face. He looked no older than thirty, but she knew that wasn't the case, 'And how elderly are you?'

'Zimmer frame elderly.'

'How does that translate in numbers?'

He shrugged, 'Really fucking old. We still age, very slowly, all Influences- even messengers of Death, which is weird 'cause we had to die in order to get this role... ' He leaned back on the ledge, looking up at the ceiling, 'They think I was just a kid. Maybe just twenty. And that was... 1915.'

Haidee's jaw dropped as she did the maths, 'So... you're, like 124?'

'And no wiser now than I was then.' his words were filled with regret, 'I think it might sound like I won the lottery, but I haven't. All this time, but I'm not free to do whatever I want with it. I have no family, no friends and no life to live. Just time.' The pity in her eyes made him uncomfortable, 'I didn't mean- I'm fine. I have a role and I'm alright with that- and just didn't want to pour salt in the wounds...'

The truth of their circumstances tightened the tension that had eased between them. Haidee wouldn't allow it to worsen.

'Tom.'

'What?'

'I'm calling you Tom.'

'Any particular reason?'

'Nope.' she chirped, 'Does it need one?'

'No, I guess not.' He offered his hand to her, 'Nice to meet you Haidee, my name's Tom.'

The last few days had changed her entire perspective of the man sitting beside her. She shook his hand. It genuinely felt as though they were meeting for the first time, which is why she could say in all sincerity, 'It's nice to meet you too, Tom.'

She continued to quiz him, getting to know more and more about him. He didn't have a home and when he slept, it would happen in an instant, causing him to vanish and reappear in the first place he thought of. Eating was unnecessary but enjoyable. The coat he had been wearing, along with a few other of his clothes, he had claimed from a black bag thrown out by a scorned woman looking to make her cheating ex feel like the trash he was. When it came to buying anything, it was with change he found on the streets. Whenever he saved up enough, he would treat himself to a sausage supper which he would eat on Portobello Beach while watching the sunset. Haidee commented on how jealous she was, him living life rent-free.

She learned that animals could see him, even when he chose to be invisible to people. He wasn't a dog or a cat person, but a fish person which Haidee found hilarious. She announced that she too was a fish person- of the battered variety, which ignited a jokingly-heated debate.

Tom then guessed that Haidee's favourite colour was red only to discover that it was her least-favourite colour, despite wearing an almost-red dress to the ceilidh. Her favourite colour was teal, though it never suited her. His was yellow, unfortunately he struggled to find a nice yellow jumper.

The hostess urged people to return to the dance floor, adding that it was time to make things more festive. The pair of them rushed downstairs. Without thinking, Haidee had grabbed his hand to lead him to the dance floor. It was only when she saw his expression that she had realised how it was a curious thing to do. Still, she did not let go.

Instead of the normal instrumental jig music, the band was covering classic Christmas tunes, most of which weren't designed to complement Scottish country dancing. Mayhem ensued as people struggled to keep the rhythm, misstepping and running around as they tried to find their place. It was the best kind of chaos, everyone was having a laugh.

Of course, *The Proclaimers* were covered. It may not be a Christmas song, but Haidee was convinced that it had become an unwritten Scottish law that *500 Miles* had to play at every event that claimed to be even remotely Scottish. Every conscious person in the vicinity sang along, from the drunken grannies to the young children who didn't even know the actual lyrics.

'We're almost at the end of the ceilidh folks,' the hostess said at ten to ten, 'We couldn't have celebrated Christmas Eve without this all-time favourite song, but being as it's not your usual ceilidh tune, we'll have to do a little improvisation on this one. So, if you just want to sway during the intro, I'll trust you'll know when to start.' She knowingfully grinned at the participants then quickly went over the steps to The Gay Gordons.

It was a simple partner dance, no grouping required. Haidee and Tom stood patiently for the song to begin. It was slightly more intimate than the other dances; they had their arms around one another, both hands in a delicate hold beside her waist and above her shoulder. The gap between their bodies was a narrow one.

The piano chimed out twelve nostalgic chords. Both their faces lit up with joy. Fairytale of New York by The Pogues and Kirsty McColl. They began to sway, as did everyone in a full circle. Haidee's back overlapped with Tom's chest as they swayed in each other's direction. As they eclipsed she felt two faint thuds against her back. She swayed away from him then back together and lingered against him long enough to feel three thuds.

It was a shock, although it shouldn't have been a surprise. His name was Tom. He wore jumpers constantly. He was a fish person. His favourite colour was yellow. He could eat dozens of sausage rolls. He was a person. Of course, he had a heartbeat.
She turned to him and saw that he was pulling very dramatic faces, mouthing along to the singer's voice. She burst out into giggles which were contagious to him, but he persevered with his skit.

The other instruments joined in, a cheerful beat began and the dance started, although very unevenly. The hostess had to clap along in the beginning to help people keep to the rhythm. With the female vocalist now singing, Haidee had her bash of lip-syncing.

They took four steps forward and, with a quick twist of both arms, they flipped themselves to face the other direction while taking two steps backwards. They repeated the same action then Haidee twirled three times under his hand as they moved forward, until they met in a waltz position and burled around the room. They repeated these steps again and again, and this was the dance of The Gay Gordons.

While their bodies had found their routine in the steps, Haidee and Tom were having a merry time mouthing along to lyrics. As the merriment continued, their voices made an appearance. No longer were they just mouthing along. They were singing; they were singing a duet.

Towards the end of the song, the tone turned melancholy again, within her heart as well. The fondness she felt for Tom was genuine and it was only a matter of time before the truce had to be broken. In the grand scheme of things, he had a role to play and she could not accept that the role was her reaper. With that thought, she called upon her logic to help desaturate her doubts so that she could see things in black and white. All her logic did was help her to see every shade of every beautiful colour, a rainbow of reasons why their circumstance was not so simple.

The worst part was, when she couldn't paint him as a monster in her mind, she actually understood why he did everything that he did. He was a threat to her very existence and, without consciously deciding to do so, she had forgiven him for it.

She couldn't stop smiling. He couldn't stop smiling. The song had reached its instrumental outro and people were repeating the steps, which the pair of them had completely lost track of.

Tom fumbled with his feet for a second, 'What do we do?'

Haidee grabbed his hands and placed one on her waist, 'Polka!' She giggled and began to burl again, 'When in doubt, polka.'

They spun themselves dizzy until the music stopped.

CHAPTER 21
Go Tell It On The Mountain

It was twenty-two minutes until Christmas.

The ceilidh had ended with the song Loch Lomond, uniting everyone in a circle, joined hand-in-hand. Guests had poured out onto the streets of Edinburgh, some stumbling into taxis, others choosing to walk home. Tom and Haidee said goodbye to the old couple who had parked not too far away.

As Haidee and Tom began to walk, she said 'Thank you, for the truce.'

'You're the one who suggested it,' he smiled with a bittersweet taste stuck between his teeth, 'I'm grateful.'

She nodded awkwardly, there was a part of her that was ashamed of her newly-found predilection of him and this urged her to make her journey home alone. 'I guess I better be go-'

'I'd like to show you something.' he said earnestly, 'It's just across the road.'

Despite him now being likable, that didn't automatically make him trustworthy, 'It's not... You're not gonna do anything...'

'It might be a bit bizarre.' he admitted, 'But it's not harmful- in any way. It might be a wee bit shocking at first.'
'What is it?' She was even more wary now.

'Well, it's a who, actually.' He nodded his head towards a close off of the Royal Mile, 'You don't have to come.'

She was aware that she didn't have to, but she had become curious. With some apprehension, she followed him through the dark and narrow archway. A faint light beckoned them into an open space, walled in by looming classic buildings. The light was held within an old Victorian lamp that stood in the middle of the court. Beneath it, standing in the thin blanket of snow, was a fox. It stared at her, unafraid.

Tom walked closer to it, watching Haidee's face the entire time. She too was unafraid. Crouching at its level, she stretched out a hand for it to sniff. It stayed put, only moving its tail to show that it was not fazed by her presence.

'What do you see?' Tom asked.

She looked at him, puzzled, 'A fox, obviously.'
His head fell to face the ground in disappointment.

She raised an eyebrow, 'Why? What should I see?'

He raised his head, not to reply but to continue observing Haidee and the fox.

She shuffled her feet closer to the animal, not worried that her hand was just a bite away from the creature's teeth. Certain that the fox wouldn't harm her, she raised her hand and placed it on its furry head.

It should have been furry. It should have been warm. Yet, her palm felt empty. Her hand fell through the creature's form, rippling its appearance in the air until she yanked her arm back.

She cursed in surprise and turned to Tom for answers. The answer he gave was a little laugh and nothing more.

'It's not a ghost.' she stated, looking back to the fox and acknowledging that lack of icy feeling she had felt with the previous ghosts she encountered, 'Unless animals are different?'

'No.' He offered a hand to help her hand, 'He's no ghost.'

'Then what is *he*?'

'Death.'

'I thought you were Death?'

Looking flattered, he shook his head, 'Yes and no. I'm the one who does the grunt work. I guess you could say he's my supervisor. We're the Edinburgh department. Just me and him.'

'You and a fox?'

A little knowing smile appeared on his face, 'That's what death means to you.'

With a curious tilt of her head, she questioned this.

'Death appears however you perceive it. I see a ghoulish wraith. Classic hooded Grim Reaper. Think I read a little too much Charles Dickens when I was alive. Never been able to communicate with him, Arthur and Estonia could. Arthur saw a Jacobite and Estonia saw a wee boy. Was hoping you'd be able to see someone you could talk to. It's strange that you see a fox.'

It wasn't strange in the slightest. Haidee knew exactly why she perceived Death as a fox. Although a grandparent had died when she was very young, but old enough to remember, the first time anyone had explained death to her was when she found a dead fox.

Six years old, running in the forest on a family walk, just having had a picnic by the side of a river. Eager to explore, she had ran ahead of her parents and saw the puff of orange fur at the base of a tree. Being an admirer of all things fluffy, she sprinted to pet it, but stopped her hand just before it reached its fur. It was like a rug, its fur fluffed up but its body flat against the dirt. Its eyes were wide but completely vacant, staring past the river, trees and existence itself. It frightened Haidee into a trance, she could not look away no matter how unsettled it made her.

It was her dad who picked her up and took her away. She remembered looking over his shoulder to see her mum lay down some freshly-picked daffodils beside it. As she rose back up, she looked to her with a smile and caught up with them, giving her the one flower she had kept.

"It's in heaven now. No need to worry."

"It looked in pain." Haidee had said, her mind focusing on the fox's expression.

"No, no. It's not in pain. It's not in its body anymore. It's lived its life, it's done all it needs to do, and now it's moved on. That left behind, it's like its clothes. Like a suit."

"What I saw was just a suit?"

"Yes, honey-bun. Just a suit that the fox didn't need anymore."

As her focus returned to the present, she felt a bit puzzled, 'Why is it just you and him?' she asked, 'What happened to Arthur and Estonia?'

Tom tried to cling onto his smile, but the warmth behind it had gone cold. 'Everyone dies. Even him-' He pointed to the fox, 'Even me.'

'But you said you already died.'

'Aye, but we were given a second life to play out this role. Even that'll come to an end.'

'And you brought me here, hoping he could talk me into... ending?' Despite the accusation she laid at Tom's feet, there was no anger in her words; only kindness that shone through her sadness.

Tom shuffled his feet, circling the lamp post as he stared into its light and pondered. He wondered if he had become a tool for Death, rather than the maintenance man. While he knew it wasn't his conscious intention to have his higher up do the influencing, he questioned if he was just instinctively searching for last resorts to move her on.

The truth was something he could never admit to himself. While it wasn't the first time he had talked to the living, became familiar with one and celebrated amongst many of them; it was the first time he felt truly fond of one. He didn't have to lie, he didn't have to hide away his identity, she knew him for what he was; good and bad. The reason he had brought her there was because he wanted to share a part of his life with her, the part he never got to share with anyone. Tom wanted her to know him better.

'Merry Christmas.' Haidee's voice pulled him out of his daze.

She was standing right in front of him, with a smile on her face brandishing her phone. On the screen were four zeros in a row. It was officially Christmas.

'Merry Christmas.' he tried to say, but it came out almost like a whisper.

'Can we keep the truce for tod-'

'Of course.' he cut her off in a fluster, 'I'd like that.'

'Good. Then can I ask for a present?'

He scoffed, 'Well, uh, all the shops are shut and I wouldn't know what to get you.'

'But you can make me anything I want right?'

He stared for a moment not sure what she was implying.

She tapped her left temple twice, 'Up here.'

The truce had surpassed the basic mutual trust. It was astonishing to Tom that she would willingly invite him into her head, when her sheer will had managed to push him out before.

'What can I do for you?' He asked.

'A dragon, please.'

He erupted into laughter, mostly out of disbelief over her eagerness, 'What a demand.'

'Well, are you gonna deliver?'

'Already have.'

Her eyes followed the direction of his finger up to the sky. Spiralling down to meet them was a winged reptile, no bigger than a West Highland Terrier. It glided gracefully towards the lamp post, perching itself sideways on the pole.

'Is it a friendly dragon?' Haidee asked, although she was already walking towards it, hand out to pet its viridian scales.

'Dunno, haven't met him.'

'Ha, ha.' Haidee rolled her eyes and then brought her fingertips to the creature's nose, as a way of introducing herself.

It gave her hand a sniff, and not two seconds later, the dragon nudged its head into her hand urging her to pet it. She did so as if it were a dog, tickling behind the ears, scratching its neck and rubbing its belly. It responded just as any playful pup would.

Tom watched as she played with her gift, cuddling it, trying to teach it fetch with an empty can of Guinness she found in the close, throwing the creature up in the air and watching it take to the sky.

As it danced above their heads, she turned back to him. There was a question in her eyes but she wouldn't ask it. She didn't have to. Tom knew, but wouldn't dare to answer it. That is, until she plucked up the courage and opened her mouth.

'There's a limit.' he swiftly said before she could get a word out, 'To what I'm willing to do, there's a limit. I've already put you through enough.'

'But it would make me happy.' she pleaded with a teary-eyed grin, 'I just want to see her, just for a bit.'

'It wouldn't be her.' Tom walked towards her and rubbed her arm, 'I'd be writing the script. What you'd see is a puppet. Not your mum.'

Haidee twisted her lips, stretching her cheeks this way and that, as if it would help massage away the tears that were brewing. Then, she nodded and composed herself with a sigh.

'Can I ask for one more thing then?'

'Certainly.'

She wiped away the wetness from her eyes and let out a laugh, 'All this time in Edinburgh and, you know what? I have never ever been to the Pentlands.'

He shrugged, 'Hiking is not everyone's cup of tea.'

'I've always wanted to.' She clasped her heart, 'Can we go? Can you take me there?'

Tom placed both hands on her shoulders. Branches of light flickered into existence, rising from his back and doming around them. With a flash, they were standing on a thick bed of snow. Grass tickled up their legs all the way to their knees. The darkness had swallowed the world up, but Tom's lightning bolts radiated for long enough for Haidee to see the rolling hills garnished with trails of purple heather and a reservoir glistening in the moonlight.

As his light faded, she turned to see Edinburgh. It was a sea of stars, a galaxy fallen to earth, but the blackness of this space had a border. She could make out perfectly the silhouettes of Edinburgh Castle, of Arthur's Seat, of the Walter Scott Monument, of everything she knew of home.

'What now?' Tom asked, excited at her excitement, 'Do you want a midnight tour? A sledge down each and every hill?'

'I just wanna sit.' She beamed back at him before throwing herself down on the snow, 'I just wanna sit and watch the sunrise.'

'It'll be a while.'

'I know.'

He sat down next to her and watched the night slowly crawl away, making way for the sunrise that burned on the horizon. They spoke about everything, but nothing in particular; just a blether as if it were between two old friends, catching up on life. It was the first time in her life she watched the sunrise, and her face lit up just as the sky did. She tried to fight back sleep, wanting to watch the sun take flight off the horizon into the cloudless blue sky. It looked like Christmas Day was going to be a beautiful day.

Tom was glad to see her happy, and relieved that she wasn't suspicious of him. He had painted over reality's endless grey sky that was only dimly lit by the sun hiding behind the clouds. She said she wanted to watch the sunrise; he made sure she did.

As she drifted off, unable to push back her tiredness any longer, he began to sing. It was a familiar tune, but she could barely make it out. He sang so quietly that his voice drifted like a breeze, travelling with her to her dreamworld.

She caught a word, just one word before falling asleep:
heather.

CHAPTER 22
Merry Xmas (War Is Over)

This is how Haidee McLean spent Christmas Day: It started with an hour-long phone call to her dad, connecting more over the phone than they had done in person in years. She brought up previous Christmases and embarrassing childhood memories. She even managed to talk to Moira for a good ten minutes without any awkwardness on either end.

The next thing she did was make phone calls to Leah and then Matthew wishing them a merry Christmas. She told them an edited version of the previous night, in which she went to The Hub solo and partnered up with a man called Tom whose parents had dragged him along. Leah baited her with suggestive noises, accusing her of forming a romance on Christmas Eve. Haidee assured her it wasn't like that. It would have been easier to convince her if Haidee could reveal who Tom really was and what he did.

After phoning those closest to her, she messaged the rest of her friends, even finding ones she had lost touch with on social media and reconnecting. The first present she unwrapped was from her father. She pulled it out from under the little tree, which she had now eaten all the decorative chocolates from. Beneath the paper she tore through, there was a box; within the box was a square of polystyrene that sprinkled off little beads like snow across the floor; within the polystyrene square was a snow globe; within the snow globe was Edinburgh Castle. She shook it up and gazed at the fake snow fluttering down around it. Home sweet home.

Later, she rolled up her sleeves and deep-cleaned the flat. The polystyrene was erased from the carpet, along with crumbs, fluff and random bits of thread. The kitchen sparkled, the bathroom gleamed and two pound eighty three pence was retrieved from the depths of the couch cushions. While cleaning is not how many people would want to spend their Christmas Day, she wanted it to be clean for Leah and there was no other time to do so.

An alternative Christmas dinner: breaded turkey steaks, a mixed bag of vegetables and roast potatoes. There was too much to fit on one plate, which is how she intended it to be. She placed two meals down onto the table, settling them on two placemats.

She sat in front of one of them, keeping her hands on her lap and staring off into the distance patiently. The idea to put the meals back in the oven to keep them warm was currently crossing her mind, until the nagging feeling had returned, just as she had hoped.

'Take a seat.' She gestured to the chair opposite her.

Tom appeared but he stayed beside the window, feeling it best not to warm the seat, 'Are you expecting someone?'

'You.'

At first, he thought she was pulling his leg, until he remembered that she had no one else. All her friends were at home with their loved ones, and she was stuck with Death.

Feeling impatient, she tucked into her turkey steak, 'It'll get cold.' she warned.

The smell of the food lured him forward, his tongue salivated in preparation for the taste. His feet stopped themselves from going any further.

'I didn't come here to eat.'

'Well, surprise! I've cooked, so the polite thing you can do is eat it.' She waved at the seat, urging him to sit down, 'I'm a good cook, honest. I mean, the steaks I just bung in the oven, but nothing is burnt.' He still looked unsure, 'It's not poisoned. I doubt that'd kill you anyhow.'

With that, he caved in and was eating by her side seconds later, 'Thank you.' he said with his mouth full. 'You're welcome.' she said with her mouth full.

The tension between them kept tightening and relaxing sporadically. A sudden accidental meeting of the eyes triggered them to concentrate on their meals with more attention than they had ever given any food. Tom danced peas around his plate before scooping them up and devouring them. Haidee took little nibbles of her turkey steak, savouring it. Both did so to buy more time.

'Are we on Cinderella time?' she spoke after twenty minutes of silently eating, 'Does the truce break at midnight?'

Tom had finished his meal, leaving a final few peas on the plate. He never actually liked peas. 'It depends on how you look at it.' He shrugged, then became uncomfortable in his chair, fidgeting with his hands and moving around in his seat. 'I came here today for a reason-'

'I know.' Haidee sighed and leaned back in her seat, 'It's okay.'

'It's not, you don't know-'

'It's okay.'

'No it's not.'

'Tom!' She said his name loudly and firmly, as if trying to gain the attention of a misbehaving child.

Reaching across the table, she took a hold of his hand. He looked ready to crumble. Despite raising her voice,

Haidee was the calmest she had ever been around him, completely poised with a small smile on her face.

'It's okay.' she repeated, 'I'm okay now.'

Disbelief caused his expression to fall into a vacant stare. Her tranquil manner and the softness of her words couldn't possibly mean what he thought it meant.

'I'm ready to die.'

He snatched his hand away and fell back in his chair, his eyes searched the air for answers. This was not the reaction she was expecting. The silence stiffened them. She watched him watch her, his eyes narrowing down her reflection in his eyes. The thoughts racing in his mind were so fierce and loud she could almost hear them. He couldn't possibly be thinking what she thought he was thinking.

He said something that was obscured by his heavy breathing and after realising Haidee didn't understand him he repeated, 'Take it back.'

Astonishment muted her, she could only mouth, 'What?'

'Take it back and you're still protected.' He was serious, 'If you don't, even a touch of a hand and I can take you.'

It took a while to remember how to speak and even then her words staggered on as they left her mouth, 'That would be the point.'

He abandoned his seat at the table, charging to the corner of the room keeping his back to her. She could hear him steady his breath. She could see him drag his hand over his face. The branches of light were faintly coming into view acting as a veil between them. Then he turned, the bags under his eyes had specks of moisture and his face was turning red. She stood up, to level her eyes with his, to look into him, to try and understand.

'I don't want to.' the voice coming out of his mouth was like that of a frightened child, vulnerable and overwhelmed, 'I came here to tell you that. I don't want to.'

'I know you don't want to.'

'No- no.' He began to laugh, a laugh with no amusement, 'I *won't* take your life.'

Delight ignited within him, diminishing his anguish. The weight of the world had lifted from his shoulders. Haidee's stunned expression had frosted over. She could find nothing to say nor nothing to think. For a moment, all she was, was quiet.

Then, when she did speak, it was filled with bitterness, 'Well that's just peaches and fucking cream, eh?'

This was not the reaction Tom expected. She walked to the window, trying to distract the rage that was beginning to brew in her with the sight of pretty little snowflakes floating on by.

'Haidee...' He said her name in a plea to face him. She didn't. 'I'm telling you, you can live a full life.'

'What was the fucking point then!' She stormed towards him, 'You had a choice this entire time?'

Feeling she was dangerously close to him, he backed away. 'It's not that simple-'

'It is!' She shrieked, 'You held a goddamn knife against my throat!'

'I'm sorry!'

'Sorry?' Tears erupted from her eyes, 'I was ready to die! I wanted to die- I want to die!'

'No you don't!' He shook his head, her tears contagiously evoking his own, 'You don't.'

'You got your wish! It all worked! I can't handle it anymore!' Her back fell against the wall, her vision blurred by tears and her head disorientated by the distress.

'I'm not going to put you through any more!' he cried back, 'There are consequences for this, I'm not meant to have a choice- but this isn't just about you. I don't want to be anyone's nightmare! I don't want to be made to do the things I'm made to do!'

She turned to him, arms flailing, 'Just do it- you said it yourself, I'm meant to be dead!'

'So am I!' Her eyes widened struggling to comprehend what he was meaning, 'I died. I died. In fucking 1915!' He brandished his smooth, ageless hands, 'That's how I became an influence of Death, I died unafraid of death! But I'm afraid of it now. I'm afraid of what I am asked to do. And I don't want to spend another second of this long agonising life hurting you- it hurts me too- I can't do this- I won't do this- It's not fucking fair! Take it back! Say you want to live!'

She was too stunned to say anything.

He wailed harder, 'Take it back!'

'I take it back.' she whimpered, 'I want to live.'

They stood together, and cried together, for a moment before the shock of it all pushed them into each other's arms.

It was surreal and unreal as she clung to the man who had been trying to kill her for the past month. One thing brought them both solace: this misery was over. Haidee McLean would live.

Still holding her tight, Tom asked, 'What do we do now?' Haidee's shaken nerves produced an all-too-familiar craving, 'I think there's only one thing we can do.'

A small vapour left Haidee's mouth and slithered into the cold night air. Leaning out the window, she tapped the end of the spliff and watched the burning ash fall before passing it to Tom. A brisk inhale was all it took for him to cough up the smoke. She laughed as he slumped back into the couch that they had pushed against the window.

The weed was from Leah's stash; she wouldn't mind Haidee treating herself to a very merry Christmas. It did a good job at calming the nerves, although Tom was struggling to hold the smoke in his lungs.

As the joint came to an end, she stubbed the remaining flare out in the ashtray and looked at Tom. With a worn-out ashen complexion and sunken eyes, he was hardly a model for youthful appearance but he didn't look old. He had said himself, he was barely an adult when he died.

'How did you die?'

He lazily rolled his head to face her, 'I can't remember.'

'No marks or anything?'

He shook his head. Haidee kept pestering him, feeling more comfortable around him now that he had decided to spare her life. She managed to persuade him to tell her his life story, the life he remembered.

First thing he remembered, he was sitting in Princes Street Gardens with a man beside him. The man asked him to reveal the first place that sprung to mind. He replied, "Corstorphine." and the man told him that Corstorphine would be his name onwards. That man was Arthur.

He spoke about meeting other Influences throughout his time. He had met Faith very early on, commenting on how he had always been a "shit-stirrer." He had been approached by a woman called Niamh, who revealed herself as an influence of fear and asked for his help on several occasions. This Niamh had been responsible for Haidee's nightmare tour of Edinburgh, in which the Walter Scott Monument fell. She owed him more than a few favours.

He went on to explain how humans qualified to become Influences. For Faith, their faith had to be so strong that it transformed belief into knowledge, that despite no evidence, what they had believed in was fact, in their minds anyway. Hope had many Influences, as they met their qualifications by holding hope in the most hopeless circumstances. Two world wars recruited a lot for Hope. They also recruited a lot for Fear, as it took people who, despite being petrified, overcame their fears.

Shame took the guiltiest who succumbed to their conscience, murderers and rapists who confessed with no provocation. Obsession took those who dedicated their lives to a singular passion.

Then, Tom started to detail how Influences are bound to certain areas. Depending on the influence, the wider the area. For Death it was as narrow as could be, assigned to certain cities and counties. He died in Edinburgh, therefore he could not leave the capital.

'Which is why you need to leave.' he added.

Haidee looked offended, 'Why?'

'Like I said, there are consequences.' He gazed off out the window, 'The minute I tell Death I won't take your life, he'll come after you. If you leave, none of the other Deaths will bother you, not with Faith's mark on you. You're only Edinburgh's problem.'

She gazed at her snow globe, to the miniature castle. *Edinburgh's problem*: a phrase that fractured her heart.

'I can't come back?'

'When you're old and grey and ready to go, you can come back here.'

She could feel a tear form and slide on her swollen lower eyelid, 'Will you be here to cross me over?'

He paused for a moment, 'Maybe. Yeah.'

'Not aged a day?' She wiped her tears away.

'Maybe by a few days.' He smiled back.

'My friends are here.' She shook the idea of leaving from her head.

'If they're really your friends, then they'll visit you.'

'My home is here.'

He held her hand, 'No. Your death is here. There are so many wonderful places out there. You'll find another home.'

Her agreement was hidden in her silence. She could not argue with him, if these were the conditions to keep her life, so be it.

'It would be safest if you left as soon as possible. You can go to your dad's, right?'

'Yeah.' she said faintly, imagining her dad's joy if she showed up at their door.

It was decided. After a long hour of packing, when her high had dropped to a low, she slept on Leah's bed, knowing it was the last time she would be in her friend's flat. She cuddled into Leah's fleece blanket that held her scent.

What felt like a moment later, Tom nudged her awake telling her it was time to go. It was seven in the morning, she had slept for six hours yet felt like she had only blinked from the last time she was awake.

Edinburgh was deserted, no buses, no cars and no people. Just them, the snow and the footprints they left behind. Haidee made sure to memorise every brick of every building, every statue and every advertisement in every window. She burned this last image of home into her eyes, so that she could see it whenever she wished.

An hour walk wore away at her legs. Tom had offered to do his speed-of-light form of transportation, but she was set on holding onto these last moments. He did the least he could do: take her large and heavy suitcase. After a quiet journey to the bus station, he passed Haidee her luggage and memorised her face in that moment, living, breathing, forming a smile.

'Thank you.' she said.

He swayed his head slightly to deny any thanks and gleamed at her with all the hope in his heart, 'Do you forgive me?'

She hummed and juggled her head side to side before giving an eventual nod. She waved him into a hug. He squeezed her tight, lifted her feet off the ground and let her back down after she let out a little tired laugh.

'I'll see you again when I'm old and grey, then.' She grinned.

'Looking forward to it.' He smiled back at her.

With that, she left, climbing up into one of the few buses scheduled that day. Through the window, he watched after her as she settled into her seat as the bus pulled out. His eyes called to her, hoping that she would still feel that nagging feeling, telling her that he was watching and wishing she would look back at him. She did.

Just as Haidee McLean was about to disappear from his sight forever, she turned her head and gave him one last smile, full of kindness, gratitude and forgiveness.

CHAPTER 23
Mary, Did You Know?

The interior of St. Mary's Cathedral was similar to St. Giles', with its stone bricks and wide arches. However, while shadows found it easy to dwell in St. Giles', the light flowed through St. Mary's easily, as if the sunlight had come to pray with the congregation.

It was easy to tell, by its smooth clean bricks and colourful decor, that this cathedral was younger. There was an age difference of just over seven and a half centuries. While Tom preferred it in terms of aesthetics, he felt just as unwelcome as he would in any other church in Edinburgh.

He sat in a middle pew, staring up at the windows above him that passed light from one another, leaving streaks of brightness overhead.

The face of Faith came into view as he stood over him, 'I sense that our mutual friend has left Edinburgh.'

'Aye.'

'Clever girl. It may be some time before she decides to come back. I suspect you'll have that name on your arm for a while longer.' Faith patted Tom's shoulders, 'But I'm not sure I'll ever want to remove my signature.'

'There's no need. She's gone.'

'Well, she understands, she'll have to die some time. There will be a day when she returns, with the sole intention of being at peace. You'll see the day.'

Tom slumped his head down.

'She can't live forever-'

'I know.' he said, 'Nobody can.'

Faith stared at the way Tom's body was limped over itself, slouched exhaustedly. The way he was speaking had risen questions and the answers were displayed in Tom's frail movements. His back inflated with each breath that was inhaled too deeply but never satisfied the hunger for air.

Faith rarely felt anger but, when he did, Influences of Death would always be the cause. Frustration cultivated within him, both at and for Tom, 'Eejit.'

Tom didn't have the energy to react to his insult. Truth be told, he agreed with it entirely but as illogical as a decision it was to allow Haidee her life, he did not regret it.

'You've seen, first hand, the price you'll pay.'

'I know.'

'Have you told Death?'

'Yes, before I came here.'

'To tell me?'

'To thank you.'

Faith took a seat in the pew in front and stared at Tom's pathetic form, 'You're delirious.'

'If you hadn't kept that mark on her, I would have killed her. It would have ate me up inside. This isn't who I am.'

'And now you've made a choice that will eat you outside in! You're an influence of Death, that is exactly who you are and what you are meant to do! Haidee McLean survived by a miracle I gave her and kept out of spite. I thought she would move to get away from you eventually, I didn't think she would submit- but you knew what you had to do if she did!'

'I don't have to do anything.'

Faith was unable to have his eyes on Tom's weakening body any longer, he looked to the floor and let out a deep breath, fed up with everything that had come from the night Haidee McLean should have died.

He huffed and rubbed his brow, struggling to comprehend, 'Why did you do it? If she had agreed to go, why would you convince her otherwise?'

Tom heedfully raised his head, the light washed out his face and made it as though his entire being was translucent, 'She made me realise this isn't who I want to be. She gave me a chance to be someone else for a change... She even gave me the name Tom.'

'*Tom*?'

'Aye.'

'*Tom?*

Tears bubbled in Tom's eyes as a cheerful laugh escaped him, leaving behind a smile as the sound echoed through the cathedral. Starting to understand, Faith returned his smile.

With his words released from remorse and regret, Tom said, 'We parted as friends. As pathetic as this sounds, I'm really glad I made one more friend before I die.'

CHAPTER 24

The Braes of Balquhidder

Curiosity demanded all of Haidee's attention. For the past three days she had read through every genealogy and history site she could get free access too, which was not many. She found that she could find basic information on people's deaths on *Scotland's People*, only needing to pay for the detailed documents. This would have been useful, if she had a name to go by.

Despite being released by her Watcher and reeling in the sensation of being completely alone, she could not stop thinking about him. December had changed her, opened her mind to the secrets of the world and imprinted her with a desire to know more. She wanted to know who Tom was before he was a messenger of Death.

The scraps of information she had could only get her so far: he died in Costorphine, as a teenager in 1915. Despite the little information she had, she had managed to whittle it down to 90 people that died in Edinburgh during 1915. She then cross-referenced each name through *Scotland's People*. After spending a day with her eyes glued to the computer, reading name after name after name, she turned up with nothing.

It was clear that more than 90 people would have died in Edinburgh that year. Any record of Tom had to have been buried or lost. On a whim she googled, "1915 teenager death Corstorphine".

The first four results were grim news of recent teenage deaths. The fifth blue heading hovered above the end of the page, "Shot At Dawn - Remembering Those Lost". It was as though the nagging feeling that would tell her that Tom was watching had returned. Except, this time, instead of his gaze on her, it was like his voice called out for her to find him. She followed the feeling and clicked on the website.

It was a website dedicated to the soldiers who were branded as shirkers and put to death by their fellow soldiers. Some were just boys, several of them had faked their age to get into the army earlier, not realising what a mistake they were making. If Tom was a soldier in Edinburgh, it was most likely he was part of the Cameron Highlanders infantry. There were four soldiers from that infantry. Two of them had died in 1915: James Adamson, aged 30 and Christopher Gilchrist, aged 19.

It stirred a dance between excitement and dread that had her head spinning. She struggled to prepare herself for what would happen when she clicked on the link, scared that the messenger of Death she had grown fond of had died in such a miserable way. On the other hand, she was worried that she would discover it was not him and have to accept she would probably never know who he truly was. While she was mulling it over, her curiosity had hijacked her hand and clicked for her.

She jerked back into her seat, eyes wide open, allowing the information to flow right to her brain the second it loaded onto the screen. The first thing to appear was a photo of two young men. A gasp slipped out her mouth, an audible cheer from her heart. It was hard to tell which one was him at first, as both looked much younger but so very like him.

They were in soldiers' uniforms which, for the Cameron Highlanders, included a kilt. The person standing beside him could almost be his double but his hair was a few shades darker, his nose smaller and his jaw wider. The caption revealed that this was his older brother by two years, David.

She read on, fascinated and overjoyed by the plentiful amount of detail. He was the second youngest of five children. Besides David, his other siblings were Andrew, Alvinea and Isobel.

Andrew died from tuberculosis as a child, making Tom- or Christopher- the only ones not to have children. David left behind a wife and son when he finally succumbed to his wounds two years after the War's end. Alvinea had three children and Isobel had two. Both of them lived to see their eighties.

It was the children of Tom's nieces and nephews that supplied so much information on him. They told stories that were passed down to them. He used to pest his sisters by planting sticky willies, a common Scottish weed, on their dresses. He would always make up for it with Isobel by giving her a bouquet of wild flowers.

Through the stories, she got to know Christopher Gilchrist. She learned of his gentle manner and how he always offered to help, even when he did not know what would be asked of him.

Though his manner wasn't as gentle around his family, they wrote about his mischievous pranks and how his mother went off her head when she felt her homemade strawberry jam on her toes while putting on her new pair of shoes.

They mentioned how Isobel would listen to the song *The Braes of Balquhidder* repeatedly in her old age and fall into a memory of Christopher singing his favourite song. It was this point that they wrote, "friend of Christopher's told David that Christopher hummed the song up until his death." It was believed this friend knew someone in the firing squad.

The documents and stories grew melancholy the more she scrolled down, eventually piecing together why he died: desertion. A letter to Isobel revealed all. The paper that had been photocopied was crumpled and creased and the handwriting was indistinguishable. Thankfully, they had written a transcription.

Christopher had written to Isobel detailing his inability to fight. This was not out of the fear that unravelled most soldiers' minds but the fear that one of his bullets had taken the life of another human being. He joined the military to help, thinking that the enemy deserved to die and that he could be the one to kill them. He explained how his change of heart happened as a result of a German soldier, who looked his age if not younger, grabbing his foot and begging him for help as he lay dying. He realised that they were all people, desperately trying to survive a war that they themselves had not chosen.

The plan was: for Christopher to appeal as a conscientious objector and switch roles to a medic whilst he was on leave. It wasn't that simple. They hadn't made the exchange and seemed as though they weren't going to. When his leave was over, he refused to go back. The military did not understand how he could change his mind and saw him as a deserter.

They killed him because he would not kill.

Haidee found it difficult to calm herself, her imagination forced her to watch as a firing squad riddled Tom with bullets, humming to himself while he still could. Despite not remembering who he was as Christopher, he never stopped being that person.

On his behalf, she hated that Death had chosen him and the cruel irony that he had become victim to. He chose not to kill only to have that be made his sole purpose. Now, history had repeated itself. Once more, he was told it was his duty to take a life and, once more, he would not. A new feeling had arisen within her in regards to Tom: respect.

She jumped up, caught off-guard by the ringing of her phone at six in the morning. The little energy she had was provided by her desire to know more about Tom but, now that the desire was satisfied, she was struggling to fight off the exhaustion and had no time for break-of-day prank calls. She picked up the phone to dismiss the call but hesitated upon seeing Leah's name on the screen.

Haidee answered.

CHAPTER 25
2000 Miles

It was three days after Christmas and the rain had thawed the snow, morphing it into thick brown sludge. The streets of Edinburgh were full again, with cold and irritated people getting grit stuck to the soles of their shoes.

Tom sat on a bench in Princes Street Gardens, watching workers prepare the outdoor stage, testing speakers and hanging up decorations for Hogmanay. The days were slow. He would never pass another soul on. He no longer had a purpose, it felt both liberating and tedious. He was free to sit on benches and talk to strangers with no fear of ever having to reek of death again, but had no real reason to want to spend his time with people he didn't know.

The day darkened into night and all the workers had gone home, but Tom still sat in the gardens, unsure what else to do.

Faith took a seat beside him, intruding on his time of peace, 'You look like shit.' he said.

Tom rolled his eyes. He felt even worse. Weakening day by day. 'How much longer do you think it'll take?'

'Well, you were with Arthur when he died. How long did it take for him?'

Tom reluctantly pulled that memory from the back of his mind. He had tried to forget every agonising second. 'Just over a fortnight.'

Faith nodded before sliding into silence and stared vacantly at the ground. Tom could tell that there were words lingering in his mouth, ready to be spoken. It was unlike Faith not to say what was on his mind.

'Did you just come for a visit?' Tom asked, knowing that he didn't.

Faith shook his head and his demeanor turned somewhat aloof, 'I came here on a matter of courtesy. I thought you might want to know that I have removed my signature from Haidee McLean.'

The world around them became still, bleak and distant. All Tom could see was the sly smile of a twisted man. Faith continued on without any remorse, believing he had done the right thing, and faked a sympathetic smile whilst delivering the indigestible news, 'I understand this is not what you wanted but it is how it should be. If they take her life, you'll keep yours.'

'I don't want it.' he growled hushedly, trying to stifle his rage, 'I made the best choice for her and for me- do not take that away from me!'

'A no-returns policy, I'm afraid. I can only remove a signature when she's out of my territory, but even if she was here, I wouldn't want to mark her again.' He shrugged innocently, 'She's only alive because of me. This is me, getting out of the way.'

Tom had never felt such a tenacious desire to mutilate someone as he did in that moment. The only thing stopping him from seeking vengeance at that moment was something of much bigger consequence: the life of Haidee McLean.

Electricity bolted from his back, whisking him away with a flash. He had to warn her but it was impossible for him to go to Stirling. There was only one option.

He thudded over and over again until the door opened, revealing half of Leah's violent grimace.

'Fuck off or I'm calling the polis!' she roared, bursting blood vessels in her sunken eyes before attempting to slam the door.

Tom took the impact to his foot which he had slipped in the doorway, 'I need you to call Haidee!'

Leah was stunned. She looked at him from toe to head, still in the process of waking up and unsure if she knew him, 'It's four in the morning, mate. How'd you have my address-'

'Sorry but it's an emergency!'

'I don't see any bloody buildings on fire.' She tried to nudge his foot out with her own.

'Please just call her, tell her it's Tom. She'll want to speak to me.' He hoped that last part was true.

Leah's canny-be-arsed expression evaporated into an all-knowing smirk, 'Oh. *You're* Tom.' she sniggered, 'Well if you don't have her number, she doesn't want you to call.'

'Please, it's important!'

'Aye, whatever- what kinda looney toon comes to someone's flat at *six in the morning*. Psycho!' She kicked his foot out and slammed the door.

Push had come to shove. Leah turned to go back to bed, only to see Tom appear right in front of her. She stumbled back, right out of one of her slippers, and fell against the wall.

'Jesus!'

'Not quite.' he tried to joke, but Leah was clearly the opposite of amused, 'Call her, please.'

In a state of shock, Leah shuffled her feet into her bedroom and returned with her phone already ringing.

As the ringing stopped, she pressed the phone against her ear, 'Uh, hey, Dee...'

'What's wrong?' Tom could hear Haidee say from the other side, 'Are you okay? It's six in the morning.'

'Aye, I ken... but your boyfriend's... he just appeared in my flat, says he needs to talk to you...' She held her hand up to Tom, gesturing to keep his distance and she cautiously put the phone down on the kitchen counter.

He promptly picked it up, 'Haidee, it's me, Tom.' he said stressfully, 'You need to come back now.'

'But you said I couldn't?'

'You're worse off where you are... Faith has abandoned you. Your protection is gone. You need to come back!'

Haidee felt alone, surrounded by boxes in her bedroom. She eyed up each wall, asking her instincts if there was anyone watching her. She was too scared to tell, too scared to make any sudden movements in case she was being watched by a predator ready to pounce.

'Haidee, are you listening? It's only a matter of time before the Influences of Death in Stirling are given your name. You need to get the first train back! You need to run!'

And so she did. She threw her coat over her pyjamas and shoved her feet into her shoes before racing out the door. The shoes weren't on properly until she was a good minute away. She hadn't bothered to lock the door.

She darted through the residential maze and made her way to the train station which, thankfully, was only fifteen minutes away on foot. Anxiety stayed with her for every heartbeat, shaking her to the bone with the dread that Death might be waiting for her around every corner.

The train was pulling in just as she was running across the bridge towards it. For a moment, she considered jumping down, but remembered how well that went last time. Running through the arch of the station, she heard the warning beeps of the doors as they began to close. Urgency put force in her next step, allowing her to leap through the narrowing gap between the doors, throwing herself against the other side of the train.

The only other passenger looked at her with some confusion, then continued to read their magazine. The train huffed and growled as it left the station. Haidee found a seat next to a window and tried to catch her breath. She knew she wasn't safe on a train, any messenger of Death would be able to teleport its way into the carriage in an instant, but she had other problems to solve.

When the ticket inspector came around, she had to tell a fib and make it convincing: she had a family emergency and her dad would be buying the ticket for her at Haymarket station. The inspector raised one eyebrow, less than convinced, but the early morning shift had already given them a canny-be-arsed attitude.

After that, Haidee was free to stew in her worry. If she had her earphones with her she could have passed each agonising minute quicker, but she reasoned with herself that she needed all her senses on high alert anyway.

Unfortunately, the alert was too high. Looking over her shoulder every two minutes gave a suspicious look to the, now four, other passengers in her carriage. Her chest was tight as she sat on the edge of her seat, waiting to fight for her life. Another train whizzed by- she jumped. The doors from the other carriage opened- she jumped. Her phone rang- she jumped.

It was an unknown number, but she took it having a feeling it might be Tom. Her instincts were proving to be well-refined.

'You on the train?' he asked.

'Yeah, I have been for a while- we just left Falkirk, shouldn't be more than twenty minutes.'

'Okay... If you get the feeling you're being watched-'

'Call them out, I know-'

'No.' he said, 'That only worked before because you were marked. You need to really pay attention to what you're feeling.'

It was a bombshell that blew up all confidence she had. It was an unfair fight: she was blind prey, a sitting duck, relying on the speed of that train to get into the city as soon as possible.

'Haidee?' He tried to draw her away from her flurry of anxious thought, 'You can do this, okay? You just have to get to the outskirts of Edinburgh. You're almost at the next county, and once you're in West Lothian, it'll take time for their Death to get your name. You can do this.'

'I can do this.' she said, hoping it would somehow convince her, but it couldn't shake the fear.

'Alright, I'm gonna hang up, but the minute you're in Edinburgh, I'll find you.'

'Okay...' she sighed and hung up the phone.

That's when she realised, the nagging sensation had returned. A part of her instantly doubted it, not wanting it to be real, telling herself she expected it so she imagined it. Logic kicked in, screaming she had no time to waste, it was time to run.

She ran through the carriage, banging on the button of the door to the next one. The doors gasped slowly, then opened. She rushed into the inbetween, the joining of the carriages, shaking in the narrow space. The second set of doors were even slower to open, but once they did, she wasted no time staying still for even a second longer. She ran too fast for her mind to keep up, and bashed right into the ticket inspector.

The woman yelled at her, but she gathered herself up off the floor and continued to run. Now, she was being chased both by Death and an angry ticket inspector. In the third carriage, there was only one more ahead and nowhere else to go after that. She came to a halt, no longer feeling the prickling sensation on her neck. She concentrated for a moment, wondering if they had finally entered the next county and the feeling had simply disappeared.

No. The feeling was still with her. It was right in front of her. She turned to run back the other way, only to collide with the inspector again.

'What are you doing?' The inspector grabbed her this time. The feeling was growing stronger, growing closer. The woman tried to calm her down but the desperation possessed Haidee, she shoved her to the side and ran back the way she came.

Back at square one, there was nowhere to run anymore. The nagging sensation was becoming overwhelming, Death was closing in on her. She fell to the floor cowering, wishing Tom had never told her. If she had to go, she would have rather gone in peace with her family rather than terrified on a train alone.

'Call the police for the next station.' the ticket inspector said into her radio, 'And an ambulance too.'

Haidee looked up, the woman was looking down on her, completely unimpressed. The nagging sensation was gone. There were more people on the train, looking over at her. Above the inspector's head was the screen that noted all the stops. It flickered from "WE ARE NOW ARRIVING AT LINLITHGOW" to "THE NEXT STOP IS EDINBURGH HAYMARKET."

Haidee let out the biggest sigh of relief she ever had, then proceeded to laugh hysterically in celebration.

'Is there someone I can call, hen?' the inspector asked warily, 'Where is it you're going?'

'Next stop!' she quickly said, 'I'm sorry, I'm sorry, I'm just- I dunno-'

'You're clearly having a mental breakdown, we're going to get you some help, do you want to sit down?' She gestured to one of the seats.

Haidee got up off the floor and slunk onto the chair, 'I just panicked for a moment- just- my mum had a heart attack.' Which wasn't technically a lie.

'Oh dear, I'm sorry to hear that.' the inspector said, giving the most monotone delivery of that sympathetic phrase.

'I didn't mean to bash into you, I just was having a panic attack and I didn't know where to go or what to do.'

'You're okay now?'

'Yeah.'

'You're okay to be on your own?'

'Yeah.'

'I won't need to stop this train, will I?'

Haidee shook her head. The inspector didn't look entirely convinced, but had no intention of babysitting a grown adult. As the woman left to do her job, watching Haidee from the corner of her eye, Haidee focused on returning rhythm to her breathing. The consistent oxygen eased the dizziness and relaxed her anxious nerves as much as possible. She wasn't safe yet, and every thought that ran around her mind would make sure she knew that.

Minute after minute passed. Even in the dark, Haidee began to recognise the shadows of the landscape. The thoughts in her head slowed their pace and relief washed over her- a little too soon.

The wheels let out a banshee-like screech as they fought with the rails, bringing the train to a halt. Most people were unbothered, one or two were annoyed enough to roll their eyes and grumbled. Haidee, on the other hand, was inconsolable. She ran to the door, pressing the button to open, knowing full well it wouldn't do anything.

She took a couple of steps back and tried to compose herself again. There was no nagging feeling. Her instincts weren't alerting her to any threats, so there was no reason to be alerted. The train would start again in a few minutes. There was no guarantee that the Death of this district would be given her name at this point. She had to stay composed.

After ten minutes of no movement, and an announcement of "technical difficulties" being the cause, Haidee wasn't the only one agitated. Strangers had bonded over their mutual hatred for the train services; swapping horror stories of being packed in like sardines, complaining about the state of the toilets, constant delays and last-minute cancellations.

She didn't concentrate too much on what was being said, she was far too preoccupied drafting a plan B. Her eyes scoured the area for anything that might inspire an escape plan. Lo and behold: a big red button. She spotted it on the window in the centre of the carriage. It was to be used in an emergency, the sticker below it had advised. Seconds after finding her solution, the emergency arrived.

The feeling gripped the back of her neck, squeezing tightly, raising every hair and tensing every muscle. She turned to look over her shoulder, into the pitch-black fields. The darkness was staring back.

Adrenaline flared through her system; she was already down the carriage, leaping over the table- where two bewildered people sat- and hammering her hand against the button. Intricate tiny webs of cracks broke into the glass, frosting it with damage, before it completely shattered onto the ground outside.

The two people sat there started screaming at her, but she was too busy clambering out the window to notice. As rude, inconsiderate and just down-right bizarre as they may have seen her, she didn't care. All her concentration was on running; running for her life.

The nagging feeling appeared in different places, forcing her to run in a zigzag through the field. The motorway was close by, and she knew that just a little further on that train she would have been safe. Her phone buzzed and buzzed until she picked up, out of breath, and almost out of time.

'Are you okay?' The fear in Tom's voice reflected the fear that kept Haidee running, 'I see the train has been delayed, what's happening?'

'I can't- I can't-'

Tom cursed a few times under his breath, frustrated with the little he could do, 'Haidee, what's happening?'

'I don't know! Tom- it's here- I'm trying- I don't know how far I have to go- I don't know where I am-'

'I can feel you- it's faint, but you're nearly in Edinburgh, you've got to keep going.'

She splashed right into the river, plunging her shins into the icy cold water. Her entire body was instantly numb. As she placed one foot in front of the other, she stumbled and fell with every step.

'Haidee, you can do this!' he shouted down the phone.

'I'm trying!'

'A little further, and you'll have your entire life, just push through!'

She forced the phone into her pocket and concentrated on just getting up a small mound and onto the road.

Cars whizzed by her, honking as they saw her. The white dashes in the centre of the road became her path as she ran against the traffic. Her body weeped from its fatigue, each breath she inhaled stabbed her chest and she could taste copper from beneath her tongue. Her body strained to go on but she would not stop. Through each stumble, she threw herself further forward, barely keeping her balance but refusing to fall again. Death was close behind.

Tom flashed into her sight, on the horizon with his branches of light spread out. He stood in the middle of the road, invisible to the drivers and passengers but not to Haidee. He was the goal post. He was the finish line. Seeing that gave her the motivation she needed to pick up the pace.

Tom watched in anxiety. He could see the Death of West Lothian, not the messenger, but the higher influence. At that moment he perceived Death more ghoulishly than before.

This Death was no shadow under a hood, it had a face made of tight decaying flesh that hung like rags from its skull. White hair wisped from its scalp, its boney fingers reached out for Haidee as it glided behind her, shimmering electric wings sprawling from its back.

The wings flickered, bringing Tom some relief, as it showed him that he was hindered from flashing ahead. Pride lifted his heart; Haidee must have given this Death as much of a challenge as she had given him.

The feeling of pride quickly evaporated, and dread took its place. He watched Death's hand open to catch her. She felt it. She felt the fingers grow towards her, their closeness grazing the skin of her neck. Tom cried out for her. She was already running as fast as she could, pushing each step hard into the ground to leap further forward.

Her hand reached out to him, he was inches away but so was Death itself. She felt it snatch at her, a cold touch of a fingertip as she threw herself to Tom. She landed in his arms.

Suddenly, she was numb all over. Her thoughts began to melt as her vision grew brighter and brighter. She could see Tom panic and lay her down on the wet ground. His pale face radiated and so did the sky. An instant sunrise, too bright and early for her. She didn't have any desire to move, or speak, or breath. She was happy to let the invisible sun shine the day away.

CHAPTER 26

Stay Another Day

A song. Someone was singing a song.

Haidee was in a place deep beneath thoughts, feelings and memories. The tune beckoned her to climb up back into her body and all the sensations it was feeling. The drowsiness hit her first, spinning her mind while her body lay perfectly still. Warmth was the next thing to reach her; warm air without a breeze. Her cheek was numb and pressed against a soft cushion.

As the singer's melody continued to ease her out of her unconscious state, she thought the voice and the song were both familiar. Realisation was what awoke her; it was Tom and he was singing *The Braes of Balquhidder*.

Having just woken up, her brain was still booting up, not quite running all her functions yet. She heard another voice speak, announcing that she was awake. It took a moment for her to figure out, but the singing was an echo from earlier. Her mind was briefing her on all the information it had managed to gather while she had been asleep.

Slowly, her eyes adjusted to the brightly-lit room. She scoped the area around her, noticing a desk, a bookshelf, stained glass windows and a crucifix above the door. She was lying on a cushioned bench against the wall with Faith looking unbothered on a chair next to her. Tom leaned against the wall, far from her, with a look of utter relief.

'You're in a safe place,' Faith said, 'although we're not really allowed to be back here. How are you feeling?'

Haidee made an achy noise in response.

'Well enough to get up?'

She tried not to mumble through her tiredness, 'You stopped protecting me.'

He used his usual smirk to cover his shame, 'Nothing personal, just politics.'

She looked at Tom, 'Am I alive?'

Faith laughed, 'Of course you are.'

'I thought Death caught me.'

The two Influences became very silent.

Tom turned to Faith and asked, 'Can you leave us for a bit?'

Faith was reluctant to leave but after a moment of what seemed to be silent conversation between them, an understanding was reached. Giving a courteous nod to Haidee, he left.

Tom pulled the chair a slightly further distance from Haidee before taking the seat, 'Do you remember when you... Agreed to die, and I told you to take it back? 'Cause once you agreed to go, even the slightest touch, I could pass you on?' She nodded, 'Now that Faith's protection is gone, it's the same deal... I should have realised sooner that I shouldn't touch you. If I held you for any longer you would be dead- but I promise you that you will be fine now.'

'How can I be when Faith isn't protecting me anymore? Isn't it just a matter of time before Death comes after me again?'

'I've put my signature on you.' he said, his voice relaxed but his expression tense, hinting at how difficult it was for him to do, 'Only I can kill you, which I won't.'

'That won't stop your little Fox friend though, will it? He'll do the same you did before, right? Just drive me to it?'

A few twitches of his lips gave away his caution around what he was about to say, 'I've taken care of it.'

'How?'

'It's a lot of Influence politics, the bottom line is I've bought you more time.'

'*How?*'

'I'm working it off.' he said chirpily, 'Doing extra work, it will keep me preoccupied.'

Haidee wasn't convinced by his sudden upbeat attitude, but it was clear he wanted to keep his business secret, and she was ready to be untangled from the web of Death.

'So it's over?' She beamed up at him.

'Yes. You can live, in Edinburgh, you can live a lifetime.'

'Thank you.' she said, wishing she could hug him with gratitude, 'I know you've really made exceptions for me. I don't expect that it was easy.'

His grimace confirmed that. He lost eye contact with her and struggled to make it again as he spoke, 'Haidee, I won't see you again.' He grew wary under her glower, feeling her disappointment weigh down on him and knowing that any reason he gave would be dissatisfying, 'I have no purpose with the living. You won't see me again. It's a good thing.'

'Don't you get holidays?' The joke struggled to land, being pulled down by her sorrowful tone.
They had already parted ways before but it was such a bitter idea to be in the same city and never see each other. Logically, a friendship with a messenger of Death

was not one built to last but her fondness of him grew the more she knew about him.

The information she had found sprung to mind and she became excited for him, 'Well if this is the last time I will see you, then I have some news.' Her excitement warmed a smile from him and he listened intently. She was not sure where to start, her lips began to move before her words had gotten into position. Finally, she said, 'I... Found you.'

It took a moment for him to translate her meaning. Once he understood, he became rigid, unsure how to react or how to feel.

Haidee took his silence as a sign of disbelief. 'I've seen photos,' she assured him, 'It's definitely you. I read letters you had written. There were a lot of stories about you as well, passed on by your brother and sisters. I know where you went to school and where you lived. I know your name-'

'My name is Tom.' he said, softly but with the message firm. His smile didn't break, 'That's the name you gave me, and I'm fine with that. This life has been all I've known for one hundred years. I appreciate what you've done but the life of the man you read about is gone. I think it would be too much to hear about a family and a life I don't remember.'

At first she was disappointed, but his words lingered around her until they were understood. It was not her place to tell him if he didn't want to know.

'If I can ask one thing, though.' He became nervous, 'Was I... Was I a good person, would you say?'

The desperate need to tell him everything was crushing her. She wanted to tell him how much he was loved and admired, all the wonderful things that were said about him and the pride his remaining family had for him for always trying to do the right thing.

'Yeah.' she finally spoke, the unsaid weighing heavy on her heart, 'You were a really good person. You *are*.'

His head dropped in relief. As he laughed with happiness, the electric branches began to outline him. Her heart sank.

He looked up with a smile full of life and before the blink of light whisked him away, he said, 'Thank you, Haidee.'

CHAPTER 27
Joy To The World

Haidee held onto Faith's arm as he walked her out of the church. The people inside took no notice of Haidee, not as long as she held onto him and that was the only reason she was doing so. As soon as they were out into the cemetery, where nobody was around except the dead, she snatched her hands away and put a good amount of distance between her and the man who betrayed her.

The gravestone in front of her was familiar, and looking around she realised she had been here before. It was St. Cuthbert's Cemetery, the very place where her world was turned upside down; the place where she first met Tom. She turned back to face the gravestone in front of her, it was the exact place he had been sitting when he first appeared to her. The terror that he had instilled then seemed silly now.

'Why did you take your protection off me?' Haidee asked bitterly, wondering why Faith was still hovering around her.

He rolled his eyes as if it were of no consequence, 'I should have never put it on you. I righted my wrong.'

'No. You just do one wrong thing after another- why did you put your... *Signature* on me in the first place?' Her scolding took Faith aback, 'Tom told me that you did it to... Convert my mum into your little Influence gang, but why? You must have known how screwed up this whole situation would go.'

He cackled, finding the truth in her words funny. Then, while thinking how to answer, he became very sombre, 'My plan would have gone perfectly, but Arthur got in the way. When you got sick and the doctors misdiagnosed you, your mother sensed that you were in danger. She prayed by your bedside believing that some higher power would save you and so I did. If I hadn't, she would have lost faith, maybe just for a while but then she'd be no use to me.' As Faith continued to talk about her mother, a knot turned in her stomach, 'The thing is, I only had to save you for a time. You only had to live while I was in the process of... Converting her, as you said. But making an Influence of Faith isn't easy, they don't just die and wake up an Influence, you have to detach them from their lives, and it was hard with your mum because she couldn't let go of you, no matter how many lies I fed the woman. I told her she had been chosen by God as an angel and that was why He saved you- and I still laugh at how gullible she was.'

'She wasn't.' Haidee snapped, 'If she really believed that, she would have gone with you.'

Faith contemplated her reasoning and gave a slight nod, 'Maybe you're right, maybe I did underestimate her. Maybe she even figured out what would happen the minute she became my successor.'

'You'd take your protection off me.'

'Bingo. What a smart little girl you are.' He laughed as Haidee glared back at him, 'Yes. That was my plan, you were meant to die and you would, after I got what I needed, but it took too long and-' he cut himself off, Haidee could tell there was a lot more information there, 'There were consequences.'

She wouldn't question him further. As curious as she was, she had no intentions of hearing him prattle on any longer. The guilty thoughts were consuming her, as much as she wished to blame Faith for everything, she felt as if she was the reason her mother was dead.

Faith patted her head as if he still saw her as the child he had put his mark on, 'Hush those thoughts. If your mother had lived, she'd have wished herself dead just to see you again.'

His attempt at kindness did not ease her guilt. She wanted to yell at him about how unfair it was to exchange a life for a life but that would not bring her mother back.

'With that being said...' Faith stepped backwards, the tone in his voice sharpening, ready to take a stab, 'With all the grievous things that have happened since I had given you my signature, you were not worth it.'

He grinned victoriously, watching as his words pierced through Haidee, indulging in her anguish before his branches of light rose from his back, vanishing him away with a flash.

Relief washed over her as she knew she would not see him again. She wondered if she would ever come across an influence again or if anybody else had.

Feeling bare and vulnerable from Faith's viciousness, it took some time to find the courage to move on, both emotionally and physically. While she began to walk up the steps, away from the gravestones that stared after her and towards the busy road, her phone began to ring.

She didn't recognise the number and was about to dismiss it when she felt that usual nagging feeling. Her heart leapt up as did her head, believing it was Tom. It was not. No one was watching her, as far as she could see. The number on the phone was not one she recognised, but her gut begged her to answer it.

She placed the phone to her ear, 'Hello?'

'Hello, is this Haidee McLean?'

The voice wasn't familiar, but she proceeded to answer, hoping the woman wouldn't ask her about accidents she wasn't in. It was something much better. It was a job offer. A cafe she had applied to needed someone to start immediately.

As her heart raced with excitement, the nagging feeling left her. She couldn't help but think that this was a parting gift from Tom, that he called in another favour from another Influence.

This was Hope.

CHAPTER 28

Auld Lang Syne

Leah's eyes nibbled at all of the delicious cakes she could see, her mouth watering as she could almost taste them. Haidee stood on the other side of the counter finding her friend's indecisiveness entertaining as she voiced why she was supposedly not in the mood for cake. Once the pros and cons were out of the way, she finally settled on a fruit tart because it was "healthy".

'How long now?' Leah asked while handing over the money.

Haidee passed the cake to her in a box, 'Two minutes.'

'Can ye no jus' leave?' she moaned impatiently, stomping her feet and shaking her hair like a child taking a tantrum, 'It's Hogmanay!'

'And my first day.' She laughed and smiled at Janet, the owner.

Janet waved Haidee away, 'Oh, go on then! It's no like we've got anymare customers- and this one here's annoying me, so take her with you!' She jokingly pointed to Leah who thanked her on Haidee's behalf.

The sun had almost dipped under the horizon and the last night of the year was awaiting them.

They changed clothes with careful precision in the back of the taxi. Haidee put a top on over her T-shirt then proceeded to retreat her arms like a tortoise and had Leah pull the T-shirt from the collar until it slipped off her, leaving the top on. The taxi driver kept glancing in his rear-view mirror with great concern and curiosity.

Leah then showed Haidee a list of flats to rent on her phone. The moment Haidee had received the offer of the job, she had gone to Leah's flat to tell her the good news. From there, they shared the idea of getting a flat together with Haidee crashing at Leah's once again, in the meantime. It was cheaper to split a two-bedroom between them by the prices she was seeing. With the cafe offering a lot of shifts, as two of their staff had left, it was likely she would be able to afford to flatshare by the end of the month. Of course, after planning their future together, Haidee had to give an explanation about Tom.

'He'd taken schrooms!' Leah reiterated to Dom, just after they had met up with him, Yana and Matthew, 'And I'd had ay spliff, so I wasnae much better- I literally thought he jus' appeared in ma flat!'

Haidee struggled to stay in her conversation with Matthew, distracted by the tall tale spilling over, 'Are you okay?' he asked, laying down a blanket on the grass.

They were on Arthur's Seat, with hundreds of other folk, shivering under layers of wool and cotton. They had a picnic with them full of bites, nibbles and prosecco to put in adorably wee plastic wine glasses. Haidee's homemade leek and tattie soup was the true blessing and the thermal flask was already empty.

'I'm wonderful.' She smiled, looking over the city and listening to the distant music from the concert in Princes Street Gardens.

'I'm glad to hear it.' He put an arm around to warm her. She hadn't realised how hard she was trembling, 'I was worried you'd be mad about the ceilidh.'

'It turned out really well, actually.' She returned to the memory, her face expressing its fondness.

'Really?' He pulled a funny face and gestured to Leah, who was still prattling on about her rude awakening, ''Cause, I wasn't too sure?'

'Meh.' Haidee shrugged, 'It was a good night, even if he... Does what he does and I won't see him again, it was a really good night.'

'And that's the main thing.'

For the next few hours, they drank their prosecco and blethered to strangers, laughed about the old times and enthused about the new. Then with ten seconds until midnight, as according to a man streaming the live event on his tablet, they began to count down in unison with everyone on Arthur's Seat, everyone in Edinburgh, everyone in Scotland and everyone in the United Kingdom.

Five.

Four.

Three.

Two.

One.

'Happy New Year!' the crowd sang out and began to ritually kiss, hug and shake hands.

The fireworks shot up into the air, igniting the Edinburgh sky with colours that painted the entire city and the faces of those who watched.

Haidee and Leah pulled each other into a full-on kiss before laughing and cheering manically. Then Leah spotted Matthew, awkwardly detaching himself from Yana and Dom who were passionately snogging.

She waved him towards her, 'Come 'ere, you!'

He did so obligingly and she smacked her lips against his.

'Oi, you've got some talent there!' They shared a giggle.

They all made their way around each other, hugging and pecking each other on the cheek until they were doing the same with the strangers around them.

Auld Lang Syne began to sing through the air from Princes Street, contagiously making its way through the people on Calton Hill and then to all of them on Arthur's Seat. Haidee found herself conjoined by Leah's hip, swaying between her and a man fashioning a wig made of pink streamers. She sang so loud and so strong her lungs ached and her throat throbbed but she didn't care.

She had survived Death, faced Fear full-on, found Hope and lost Faith only to find a new one.

She had faith in herself and in the people she loved. Surrounded by joy, she felt in that moment that this was her real life beginning.

CHAPTER 29
Stop The Cavalry

Haidee pulled the large case to her corner of the living room while her dad huffed, examining the mess that was Leah's flat.

'I'm not happy.' he stated.

'I have a job. Me and Leah are looking at bigger, nicer flats.' She smiled confidently, 'I'm doing good. You should be happy for me.'

'I'm happy with you home and Stirling's not too far, you could commute.' He looked at his only child, knowing that this wasn't about work or even being independent. He took a deep defeated breath, 'But Edinburgh's your home.'

Her heart filled with joy to hear her dad say that. She hopped over boxes and gave him a hug, 'Thank you.'

He nodded, shyfully, 'Well, yeah. The least I could do was bring your stuff through and visit- I haven't seen you since last year!'

She cringingly giggled at his joke. While he was technically right, it had only been a week exactly.

He left for Stirling shortly after, leaving Haidee in the flat by herself. She tried to tidy up a little as it was the only day she would have off work that week. With rustling pieces of rubbish, hoovering and moving furniture, she hadn't been aware of the new presence in the flat.

There was no nagging feeling, just a pit in her stomach, telling her there was something wrong. Something was out of place.

She froze in complete shock when she saw it. All the cleverness in her head couldn't help her to theorise as to how the hell a fox got into the flat. Dashing to the door, she tried to shoo the creature into the hallway. It would not budge. It just sat there, staring at her, its tail waving gracefully by its side.

With all that had happened now put in the past, and with a mind eager to move on, it took a few solid minutes before she would allow herself to realise what it really was in the middle of the living room. It was Death.

At first, she stayed where she was and assessed the situation. Tom had said he had taken care of everything, yet here Death was. She prepared herself for the tricks and illusions she faced in the past, but ten minutes passed without anything happening.

'Go away.' she commanded, taking a chance.

No such luck. Death wouldn't budge. She moved cautiously towards it, seeing it as no threat to her. Kneeling down, she offered her hand out as she did when she first met the creature. This was when it decided to move. It lunged towards the door, the sudden scare toppling her body over onto the floor. It waited for her in the doorway, circling itself and looking back at her.

'Do you want me... To follow?'

It ran around the corner out of sight, she took this as a yes. The Fox was waiting for her outside the flat, even as she took the time to lock the door behind her. Its gentle trots and glances back showed that it was hardly a threat to her, but being Death, she couldn't help but keep her guard up.

She followed the Fox through Edinburgh, which was clearly invisible to everyone else, strolling across Princes Street without a single person pointing it out or taking photos. It made sure to wait at traffic lights, even if the roads seemed clear enough to cheekily cross over, and despite it being no danger to him. Either way, this made it clear to Haidee that Death wanted her alive, allowing her to relax a little.

It cantered through the Christmas Market, and Haidee became distracted by all the scents that guided her nose to the sizzling bratwursts. She had some change in her coat pocket, just enough to buy one and quickly prepared to do so.

The Fox lunged at her legs, forcing her to stumble back into the couple waiting behind her, who swore at her and scolded her for being so clumsy. She was in too much shock to notice. Unlike Tom, who was as solid flesh and bone as she was, this creature's form had vanished into her legs. It popped its head out of the shins of her jeans and looked up. It stared at her until she moved out of the queue and then it bounded on its way, glancing back to make sure she followed. Death wasn't patient.

As they climbed up the steps to The Mound, Haidee had a good idea of where the creature was leading her to. Sure enough, it brought her to the place Tom had taken her on the night of the ceilidh, the first place she saw Death.

There was something in the air. A change in the atmosphere. All the noises of Edinburgh, the people, the traffic, faded out until all that could be heard was a quiet breeze and the sound of her own footsteps.

As the courtyard and the lamp post came into view, so did Tom. Her breath froze in the air. He was tied to the lamp post and blindfolded. He wasn't wearing his usual woolly jumpers or tattered coat but a soldier's uniform. She called out to him but he did not respond. His face looked softer, younger and less gaunt.

Whilst she paced up the steps, grass spurted between the slabs of concrete that had turned to mud. The lamp post twisted and mutated, turning slightly thicker and brown, the lamp melted and stretched out into branches.

Haidee turned the corner and saw five strange men of the same uniform, lined up, all with their guns pointing at Tom. Where buildings should be, there was now the view of Edinburgh from Arthur's Seat. The city was in a veil of night but the sun touched Tom and the other five men, stretching their shadows across the hillside.

She could hear Tom humming, a tune she had heard him sing twice now. He looked unafraid. He looked content with this being his final moment, humming *The Braes of Balquihidder* one last time.

'No!' she cried out, 'Don't show me this!'

She ran to his side, staring down the barrels of the rifles, grabbing at Tom. Her hands clawed right through his existence, as though he were mere mist.

'Don't show me this!' she cried in a panic.

This was worse than a fantasy. This was worse than a nightmare. This was worse than ghosts. Despite not being able to feel it, or interact with it, this was real. This happened and it happened to someone that, in this moment, she wanted to protect. She knew what was coming because it had already come and gone. She wept as she clung to him, the man who was sent to hunt her down but whose humanity prevented him from doing so, even when she had surrendered to being prey.

Her heart screamed for him, wherever he may have been. He did not deserve the fate given to him. No amount of wishing could erase the past, yet she wished she could spare his life the way he spared her's. She wished she could give him the chance for a wonderful life the way he gave her.

Christopher Gilchrist was too good. He showed mercy then and now, despite it going against everything he was and everything he had to do. He was a good man, better than the men who made the decision to take his life. He was a brave man, better than the men who stood with their guns pointed at one of their own, simply because they were ordered to. He died for having a conscience. He died for being the better man.

Bangs pounded the air, bullets flew through Haidee and into Tom. She turned to him, seeing the blood streak down his uniform, dyeing the green to black. Her hand hovered over his face, as she tried to stroke his misty form, hoping that this was somehow a portal into the past and she could give him some comfort in his final moment. She witnessed his last breath.

There was no more *Braes of Balquihidder*.

She wrapped her arms around him, only for them to pass through and hold onto something else. Ice bit at her palms. The scene had faded, she was hugging the lamp post and the only one with her was the Fox.

She moved her head so that she could have one eye on Death. It pranced around in a circle in the cove, presumably wanting to give her a tour of more grievous visions.

'I thought this was done.' she raged, 'I thought you wouldn't hurt me.'

The Fox became very still whilst Haidee stood up, trembling and snatching her breath back from the hysteria.

'This is fucking torture but it won't work! Whatever you throw at me, I have a life to live!'

She began to walk away but saw only black nothingness where the steps would be. She turned again to see Death prancing again, urging her to follow.

Determined to refuse, she stepped into the darkness and instantly stumbled. Trying to move further, she managed to steady her feet. However, the next step was just as wobbly and she quickly realised this wouldn't work for the entire walk home.

She stormed towards the Fox, eager to have its trials over and done with. It scampered onto the Royal Mile, weaving in and out of people. Once again, she suspected where it would be heading.

It stopped outside the doors of St. Giles' Cathedral. As she opened it, it dashed in and faced one of the pews which was seemingly empty.

The very few people in there took no notice of her but she suddenly took notice of Faith, who snapped into existence as he looked over his shoulder and spotted her. The Fox moved away to allow him out. He met her glare with his and strode towards her.

'It's forcing me to follow it.' she said, to make it clear she did not want to be there and she did not want to speak to him.

'Death wants you to understand.'

'Understand... Why it just showed me that?' She wiped away the wet from under her eye.

He gave a single, serious nod and she apprehensively waited for him to speak, 'The price is the same.'

She grew still, not breaking eye contact as she struggled to comprehend the meaning of what he was saying.

'I told you, there are consequences.'

'My mother's life was the consequence.' she attempted to say in confidence but her words quivered.

He smirked his usual sadistic smirk, 'Not just her's. I've kept my mouth shut for Tom, but if Death wants you to know... Then, Haidee McLean, here is the truth: your mother's life was not in exchange for yours but for another messenger of Death- Arthur, who refused to take your life even when you were in agony begging for your death, a sick bedridden seven-year-old who couldn't handle the pain- and that weakness of yours is why your mother is dead.'

Haidee's eyes widened as the puzzle pieces clicked into place; what the true consequence of a messenger of Death refusing to do their duty was. History was repeating itself.

'Arthur died because of his mercy. Death was down an Influence, and my department was punished for it. If you had been a little stronger, if you hadn't given Arthur the authority to take your life, Arthur and your mother would have had roles to play in this life, and you would be in a better place- out of the way.'

'Where is he?' she snapped, 'Where is Tom?'

Faith stayed silent but the Fox lunged towards the door. Haidee pushed the double doors open, allowing a gust of wind to send shivers down the spine of everyone inside. Darting after Death, she knew what she needed to do.

CHAPTER 30
ONE MORE SLEEP

They shot down the Royal Mile, sprinted straight down the road at the bottom of the steep cliffs under Edinburgh Castle, and reached a pathway into Princes Street Gardens. She skidded past the golden fountain, hearing a worker shout after her that they were closing the gardens, and dived into St. Cuthbert's Cemetery.

As she entered the dark, quiet, place of rest, she had lost sight of the Fox. Frantically, she searched for Tom between each grave, in every open tomb and in every dark corner. She could not see him, but she could feel him.

Relief painted a smile on her face as that nagging sensation had become one that caressed and soothed her, 'I know you're there.' She turned to face the gravestone where she had first seen him.

And there he was.

Slouched against the gravestone with those once piercing electrical branches, now limp flowing lines of light that brushed against the air. His body was frail and his face was more gaunt than it had ever been, but behind his weak form, was still the eyes of a good man.

And there she was, to put things right.

'I told you,' He could barely speak as he used the gravestone to lift himself up, 'Last time would be the last time you saw me.'

'And why the fuck was that?' She laughed in defiance of the sadness that she was feeling, 'It was because you knew that you weren't going to be around anymore.'

He bowed his head guiltily. No matter what he did, he seemed to hurt her.
She stepped closer towards him, 'That's not the way this is meant to be. You're not meant to be the one who goes.'

'I want to.' He said contently, 'I'm doing this for both of us. You'll live a great life for me and I'll be done with moving people on, I can't do this anymore. I can't move you on–'

'You can.' Tears bubbled in her eyes, 'It's okay. I'm okay.'

'I can't kill you–'

'You're not killing me.' She smiled through the tears, 'I was meant to die as a kid and I should have been allowed to. Faith should never have intervened. My mum should still be alive. You should have still had Arthur, you shouldn't have been alone. I wouldn't have been any different from that wee girl... Kaira Johnstone. Tragic as it would have been for my parents, they would have known I wanted them to move on, and they would have done eventually, and I would have been at peace. I'm not meant to be here.' She could see the agony in his eyes as she spoke and felt it as her own, 'I know you didn't want to know- but I want to tell you so badly, that you made the same choice in your first life as you're making now. You fought in World War I and realised that you couldn't kill and that is why you died. They killed you for desertion and you faced it. You didn't fear death, you'd rather die than kill someone yourself.'

Tom gasped through his own tears, feeling all that she had just said resonate in him as the truth, 'Then you understand, that I can't kill you. Haidee, you're the only person that gave me a choice in this. You gave me the chance to be human again and you have no idea how much that means to me... How much you mean to me. Don't ask me to do this.'

'I'm not asking, I'm telling.' She moved in closer, 'I said it before, that I was ready and I am. When I first met you and found all of this out, I was scared and I thought if I died now that my life would be incomplete because I haven't done all the things that I wanted to do. But I've seen and known so much more than anyone else will in their lifetimes. I've had two parents who have loved me, I have amazing friends who love me and through all the ups and downs, even when I was absolutely skint, I still managed to make the most of what I had. I was always grateful for what I had. I wouldn't change any second of it. I've lived a complete and fulfilled life. It's time for me to move on.'

He shook his head, backing away from her as she moved towards him, 'I'm not ready.'

'You are.' She nodded, 'It's okay. I'm okay, now.'

Tom was paralysed, not knowing what to do but knowing that he had to let this happen. He heard her beating heart pounding at his chest as she held him close. At first he hesitated to put his arms around her, scared she would go faster, but remembering that she was about to go either way, he clung to her, making the most of this moment they had. Her chin rested on his shoulder as she felt her body grow weaker.

After a moment, she pulled back and placed her hand on his cheek, stroking his tears away as she stared into his eyes, saying a thousand words without opening her mouth. She smiled and placed a kiss on his lips.

The bittersweet surprise caused his heart to sink even deeper. He held her waist and head, kissing back, trying to hold onto that moment for as long as possible, never wanting to let go.

Then, he felt all her weight fall for him to hold.

Moving his head back, he saw her eyes reflecting the orange lights of the street lamps but no longer reflecting the light within her.

She was gone.

CHAPTER 31
Will You Go, Lassie, Go?

As she got up on the podium, Leah felt a nagging sensation prickle at her cheeks. It was no wonder that she felt as though she was being watched when the entire room was looking at her, but it was a particular corner of the room, where nobody stood, that Leah felt a strong gaze from. She focused on that feeling, choosing to believe that it was her Dee.

She could barely see everyone through her tears as she spoke about her best friend, who was seen running through the streets of Edinburgh until her heart just gave out. Haidee's father, who sat in the front row, gripping the hand of his wife, bit his lip throughout the service in an attempt to hold back the wail building up in his chest.

Leah tried her best to smile about the good times and laugh over the best times. She spoke of Haidee's kindness, her caring and empathetic nature and how much fun she was. She went on to talk about how Haidee was always there to help but rarely accepted it herself; Haidee would tell everyone that she was okay, that she was at peace and that the only tears that were allowed to be shed for her were happy ones.

'But if it were the other way 'round and she wis up here today,' she grinned through streams of tears, 'she'd be bawling her eyes out jus' like me- total hypocrite.'

People gave a half-hearted laugh.

'But fer real...' Leah said, placing a hand over her heart, 'She wis ma best friend, *the* best friend and I'll love her 'til the day I join her, and even longer.'

She left the podium, leaving it to the clergyman and took her seat beside Matthew. He put an arm around her and clasped her hand in his as they shared their grief. Everyone showed up for Haidee, even old high school friends who had heard of the news, even old neighbours who remembered her with her mother. The pews were filled to the brim with people to the point that any guest who hadn't shown up early was standing around the sides and at the back.

Out of the corner of her eye, Leah saw Pete. This was the first time she saw him since he had stolen from her. He hadn't even shown up for Christmas, but he was here now. As they made eye contact, she could tell that her dubious brother was there with good intention. He was there for her. She gave a soft smile to show her appreciation then continued to watch the clergyman.

Tom had witnessed the power of grief tear people apart but also bind them closer together. He knew Haidee would be happy in knowing how many people she had brought together. Family and old friends were reuniting over their shared love for her.

As the clergyman finished his speech, he asked people to look at the cards given to them, which had a photo of Haidee in front of a pink hydrangea, taken that summer, looking happy and carefree before her struggles. In the card was a song for them to sing as their goodbye to her, chosen by her father, a song her mother used to sing to her as a baby.

People began to rise from their seats, and Tom felt it was the best time to leave. He had said his goodbyes and didn't wish to do it a second time- until the music began to play. One foot was already out the door, but the other stayed rooted in place. The melody was slightly different, the words similar but not the same to the ones he knew.

This was not *The Braes of Balquhidder*, but a song that had evolved from it.

It was a curious coincidence, and he couldn't help but turn around to look at everyone singing. His eyes landed on the coffin, the curtains moved themselves slowly around it. The words he knew slipped from his lips, and he found himself trying to sing along.

A cry or two from here and there broke the harmony, but through their grief, they tried their best to send her off with a song. Eventually the curtains met one another and the coffin that held Haidee was out of sight, yet the song continued.

Struggling to keep it together, he walked out the door and, in a flash, he was in the comfort of his courtyard just off of the Royal Mile.

As the light around him faded, the buildings and the streetlamps came into view, but not the usual ragged wraith that was always waiting for him. In its place, waiting under that silver light, was a woman, wearing a tartan plaid that veiled her head.

'Hello, Tom.' She smiled welcomingly.

She pulled the hood of her earasaid down, revealing her face. Fine lines tugged at the corners of her eyes and mouth. Ribbon laced through her brunette hair, keeping the messy locks bound. Her smile held a secret that her eyes gave away. He recognised the feeling of her stare. Disbelief weighed on his jaw, leaving it ajar.

She continued, 'I'm glad tae see yer strength return tae ye. I'm glad she did whit wis right.'

He stayed silent in disagreement.

'Now that I can speak tae ye, ye gone an' turn mute?' She laughed, but it soon faded out into a sympathetic smile. 'As sorry as I am, Death cannot rest. I must give ye another name, the last name I will ever give tae ye.'

His heart leapt. Death appearing before him in her true form, and offering up one name, could only mean one thing. He nodded reluctantly, unprepared for the event that was about to take place. The woman began to carve into the air, silver flames gradually writing until the name was burned in front of Tom's eyes: Elspet Moncrieffe.

Tom had always thought the last name he would be given to cross off his list would be "Death." That is all he had ever perceived her to be, so he believed that was all she was. Yet, a human being stood in front of him. All that had been taken from her was now returned: here face, her name, her true self.

'What's it like?' He asked, hesitant to do what he had to do.

'Tae be seen as ye have seen me, it can be ay lonely thing. Though, despite facing hard choices, there's ay greatness tae gifting people peace that ye will better understand, once ye remember the life ye had before.'

'How do you mean?'

'Ye'll remember aw it. Yer true name, yer kin, yer childhood- aw that ye lost, it will be returned tae ye.' She said promisingly then extended her hand, 'Now, dae me ay kindness. Gift me peace an' let us part as friends.'

He took a deep final breath of his life as he knew it, savouring the cold crisp air as it breezed into his lungs. Death waited patiently, as she had done for so long.
Then, he took Elspet's hand and shook, feeling her warmth pass through him as her existence radiated into a golden light.

Finally, Death was at peace. Now, the torch and all its burning burdens had passed over to him. Tom had become Death itself.

The life of Christopher Gilchrist seeped back to him in hazy pieces of knowledge that blossomed into memories. It all came back to him; the smell of daffodils in spring from the garden; Alvinea and Isobel tugging on his arms; the itchiness of his woolly jumpers; his deep talks with his brother David; joining the military; the heartbreak for his brother Andrew; his mum's cooking; his dad's singing; playing football with friends; dancing with girls; first time getting drunk; the carnage of the war; the pain of being shot.

It was dark. He had no idea how long his mind had been in the past, reuniting with all he had forgotten. It was as though he had been asleep and was now recalling everything he had dreamt. Becoming Death had returned his old identity but also gave him a new one.

He moved towards a window, head down, knowing he had to face his reflection but scared to see what he was now. The thought of spending centuries seeing himself as a hooded shadow, an ominous specter, squeezed at his insides.

He mourned for Haidee and wished she was there, laughing and dancing, putting him in his place and seeing a goodness in him which he thought he had lost. It felt as though he had no goodness unless she was there to see it. Without her, he could not convince

himself of his humanity, when his reflection would show him a wraith ready to reap souls.
Tom braced himself, he had to be brave. This was the face of Death as he saw it and what it meant to him; he would have to face it for the rest of his time on Earth. He looked up.

And there she was.

Haidee McLean was smiling back at him.